JAHQUEL J.

RICH *and* ROTTEN

WWW.BLACKODYSSEY.NET

Published by
BLACK ODYSSEY MEDIA

www.blackodyssey.net
Email: info@blackodyssey.net

This book is a work of fiction. Any references to events, real people, or real places are used fictitiously. Other names, characters, places, and events are products of the author's imagination, and any resemblance to actual events or places or persons, living or dead, is entirely coincidental.

Library of Congress Control Number: 2025916804

First Trade Paperback Printing: April 2026
ISBN: 978-1-957950-89-1
ISBN: 978-1-957950-90-7 (e-book)

Cover Design by Ashlee Nassar of Designs With Sass

To the extent that the image or images on the cover of this book depict a person or persons, such person or persons are merely models and are not intended to portray any character in the book.

10 9 8 7 6 5 4 3 2 1

Manufactured in the United States of America

Distributed by Kensington Publishing Corp.

The authorized representative in the EU for product safety and compliance
is eucoply OU, Parnu mnt 139b-14, Apt 123
Tallinn, Berlin 11317, hello@eucopliancepartner.com

Dear Reader,

I want to thank you immensely for supporting Black Odyssey Media and our ongoing efforts to spotlight the diverse narratives of blossoming and seasoned storytellers. With every manuscript we acquire, we believe that it took talent, discipline, and remarkable courage to construct that story, flesh out those characters, and prepare it for the world. Debut or seasoned, our authors are the real heroes and heroines in *OUR* story. For them, we are eternally grateful.

Whether you are new to Jahquel J. or Black Odyssey Media, we hope that you are here to stay. Our goal is to make a lasting impact in the publishing landscape, one step at a time and one book at a time. As always, we welcome your feedback and kindly ask that you leave a review. For upcoming releases, announcements, submission guidelines, etc., please be sure to visit our website at www.blackodyssey.net or scan the QR code below. And remember, no matter where you are in your journey, the best of both worlds begins now!

Joyfully,

Shawanda "N'Tyse" Williams
Founder/Publisher

For my Tribe

Y'all hold me down in a way I can't explain. On the days I'm tired, overwhelmed, or questioning myself, your love is the reason I keep going. This book is a thank you, a hug, a love letter. I appreciate you more than you know.

PROLOGUE

Tatiana Rich

RUBBING MY TEMPLES, I paced back and forth in front of my father's fireplace in his office, searching for the right words that would be respectful. He sat behind his desk with his hands clasped together, while his associate was seated in one of the plush chairs positioned in front of the massive oak desk—the first piece of furniture my father purchased when he built our mansion. The desk, which had many hidden compartments, was his prized possession, and he often became excited when someone complimented him on it or showed even the slightest interest.

As I kept pacing, my father's eyes followed me. I could tell he was growing impatient with my silence, but I'm not sure what kind of response he expected after having sent the helicopter to pick me up from college just so he could rip my heart from my chest and tear it into tiny pieces. I'm not saying it was his intention, but that's what it felt like.

"Tatiana," my father's deep voice thundered through the quiet room.

His associate remained seated and quiet. A much older man than my father, he was impeccably dressed, and the Rolls-Royce

Cullinan waiting outside for him told me that he had some money, which was typical for my father because he was never around anyone who couldn't offer him something.

He loved to remind me that how he grew up and how I grew up were completely different. While he grew up in New York City, I had been raised in Greenwich Pointe, a small city an hour from the Big Apple. When it came time to choose a college, my parents wouldn't let me go far. They told me I needed to pick one that was close to home, and because they had been faithfully donating to Langston-Wells University since I was a child, it ultimately became my choice. The university's new library even had my family's last name engraved on a golden plaque displayed right inside the doorway. Everyone knew who the Rich family was and the importance of my parents' contributions to LWU. So, while my high school friends were excited about picking their colleges—some even planning to study abroad—I was stuck attending a school that was almost in our backyard.

Greenwich Pointe was a prominent city filled with wealthy Black families who had more money than they knew what to do with, including my family. The lush greenery just inside the city's limits had immaculate landscaping, and a sign announced that the city was founded in 1945. Avery and Malcolm Rich moved here a year before I was born and never left because Greenwich was my mother's comfort zone. She especially enjoyed coffee dates with her friends after Pilates and was known for throwing elaborate parties that many hoped to receive an invitation to.

Unlike my father, my mother came from money, so none of what my father introduced her to was new to her. Growing up, I had a nanny, took dance and piano lessons, and never left Greenwich Pointe unless we were flying out of the country on our family's jet.

When it was time to go off to college, I couldn't wait to get out from under my parents' thumb. I was their only child, and they smothered me, always making sure I did right and avoided what I wasn't supposed to do. A teenager is expected to make mistakes they can learn from, right? Not me. I never did any wrong because that wasn't the Rich family's standard. Even now, I wanted to choose my words carefully to avoid disrespecting my father, but at the same time, let him know I wasn't going for this shit. He couldn't have possibly thought I'd agree to this.

"You called me home to tell me that I'm getting married in two months. What do you expect me to say to this news?"

My father stared at me, then glanced at his associate as I waited for him to say something.

Anything.

His associate looked familiar, but I couldn't put my finger on where I had met him before. At that moment, I couldn't care less about how or where I might have known him. I was more focused on why my father pulled me away from school.

I didn't come home often because I enjoyed my freedom at my condo in the city and relished being away from my parents. It didn't mean I didn't love them; I just liked having my own life outside of them, with friends who didn't care about the year of the chardonnay or the latest gossip in Greenwich. They only cared about their studies and living life on their own terms. Most of my friends were attending Langston-Wells on scholarships and didn't come from wealthy families.

Then there was him.

My heart fluttered whenever I thought about Nazir, who was back at my condo sleeping before he had to leave for work. I had never felt the same way about anyone else as I did with him. Although he wasn't a student at Langston-Wells, I met him there when he was visiting his cousin.

"I understand this is a lot for you to process, but you *will* marry Karim Sterling. The Rich and Sterling families have been friends for many years."

With my hand on my hip, I replied, "Well, why haven't I seen them at any of our family events? Hell, this is the first time I'm seeing this man…I think."

"Tatiana Rich, watch your mouth and show some respect. Raphael Sterling has been around our family for years. He recently moved back to Greenwich Pointe, and we both believe that merging our families through marriage will make us even more powerful."

Did I hear him right? Did he really just say he wants me to marry some stranger to make our family more powerful?

"How much more powerful do you need to be, Daddy? You're known by everyone, have friends in the highest places, and have more money than we could ever need. How much more power do you need before it turns into greed?"

He leaned forward in his chair, rested his forearms on the desk, and looked at me with a stern expression. My father was always so regal, in control, and never let his emotions show. I can't remember a time when he shed a tear or even looked like he was on the verge of doing so. He was always so stoic and commanding that being around him could be exhausting at times.

What I said was true, though. What was the point of having all this money if he and my mother weren't going to enjoy it? My parents never traveled or engaged in the kinds of activities that most people with their wealth did. With their only child away at college, I expected them to be jet-setting around the world. My father took business trips, but my mother spent most of her time alone. I think that's why she kept busy with all the different organizations she was involved in at Greenwich Pointe. It was to take her mind off the fact that her marriage was a façade; she didn't have the perfect marriage everyone thought she did.

"I'm your father, and I know what's best for you. I've allowed you to go to college and get that out of your system. Now you will return to Greenwich Pointe and marry a Sterling. And I don't want to hear another word out of your mouth, Tatiana."

"Allowed?" I managed to choke out.

My heart pounded, and my breathing quickened as I stared at my father, who had a scowl on his face, as if daring me to say something in defiance.

Raphael Sterling remained seated and unbothered by the exchange between my father and me, as if he had no doubt the marriage would happen and saw no need to intervene.

"You need to return to the city and get your affairs in order. The wedding is in two months."

Every word from my father's mouth felt like a dagger in my throat, while he seemed unfazed by it all. This wasn't ruining my father's life; it was destroying mine. Yet he didn't seem to care. How could someone be so cold and calculating?

I stood there speechless before turning and storming out of his office to find my mother, who was conducting business on a video call in the sunroom. She smiled at first, but when she saw the distress on my face, she quickly excused herself and came over to me. Her curly hair was pushed back from her forehead, with a pencil tucked into her bun, and her rich cocoa skin showed concern as she searched my eyes.

"Tati, what's going on? What's the matter?"

I struggled to control my breathing after running from one end of the house to the other.

"Ma-ma-married, Mom," I panted. "Dad's trying to make me marry some stranger."

My mother wrapped her arms around me and kissed the top of my head.

"Karim isn't a stranger. You both attended the same middle school before he moved away."

Snatching away, I glared at her and replied, "Mom, what are you talking about? He's a fucking stranger to me. You cannot possibly agree with this!"

She took a breath and gently took my hand in hers.

"Do you think your father was my first choice, Tatiana? Coming from an affluent family sometimes requires sacrifices to protect the family."

I truly felt like I was in the Twilight Zone. What did any of this mean? My father didn't come from money, but my mother did. So, what was her reason for marrying a man from a different background? I always assumed she married for love.

"Fuck what any of you are talking about. I'm not marrying him. I refuse to be used like a pawn in whatever game he's playing. He never tells us anything, and now he suddenly wants to include me in a business deal like I'm some piece of property."

"Family…we're uniting two powerful families, baby."

I snatched my hand away and sprinted back down the hall to leave. As I passed my father's office, he and Raphael were toasting as if this was going to be some beautiful arrangement.

I hated him.

"Time After Time" by Jon B.

It was past midnight when I heard the key turn in the lock of my condo. Nazir was the only person with a key, so when I heard it, I knew he was home. Although, if you let him tell it, he refused to call this his home. He said he would never feel comfortable living under a roof paid for by another man. He was prideful like that. Even though I told him I didn't need the money, he still gave me some each month to pay my father. Unbeknownst to him, I kept the money in my account, never touching it.

Despite having more money than I knew what to do with, he refused to let me spend it. When we went on dates, I wouldn't dare insult him by trying to reach for the bill or dig inside my purse for money to pay. I didn't know what Nazir was into that allowed him to spend money the way he did, and I had learned from my father never to ask. There was no reason to ask questions that I secretly knew the answers to.

As I lay on my silk pillow, I could hear him take off his boots, set his keys down on the kitchen counter, and shimmy out of his coat. I had spent a lot of time studying Nazir. He was someone I wanted to be with forever. I hoped to be his wife someday and tell our children how we met while I was in college — how their father had a plan to be more than what life had initially afforded him.

Stopping in the doorway, Nazir leaned against the frame and took a breath. Even in the dark, I knew his features as well as my own. He was 6'4" and muscular. Working out was the one thing that gave him peace and clarity. While I always felt like I was fighting for my life whenever I exercised, he did it effortlessly. His brown skin glistened as he licked his thick lips. He had a few tattoos, but had mentioned more than once that he wanted to cover his entire body in them. His hair was cut short, but his curl pattern was still visible. His beard was thick and unkempt, a testament to his dedication to his mission. To me, his outer appearance didn't matter as much as what was on the inside or his efforts to make money to take care of us.

"You're not sleep?" his deep voice grumbled, tiredness woven into his words.

I sat up in bed, and when he heard me sniffle, he moved closer.

"I can't sleep," I answered, my voice cracking.

Nazir sat down and pulled me into him as he softly kissed my lips. "What's the matter, Tata?"

He was the only one who called me that nickname, and every time he said it, I felt an intense warmth spread through my body. I've always been Tati—or Tatiana when my parents wanted to make their point clear. They had never given me a nickname, so Nazir giving me one made me feel special.

Cherished.

I took a deep breath. The last thing I wanted was to break his heart—and mine. The life we planned together wasn't just something I wanted—it was something I needed. A simple life where the man loved me the way I deserved to be loved. I didn't need jets, yachts, or all the frivolous things I had access to growing up. None of those things mattered when you're unhappy deep down inside.

My mother always looked tired and worn out, and she couldn't hide the sadness in her eyes from me. I knew her too well. I can't remember a time when she and my father kissed or laughed as he playfully smacked her on the butt. Moments like that never happened in our home. Or maybe they only did those things in the privacy of their bedroom since my mother was on the conservative side. For years, I believed that until I was old enough to realize my parents had a master suite with two sides—one for her and one for my father—like British royals.

"Let's run away, Zir."

With a confused look, he replied, "After you had me buy those damn concert tickets you wanted? We're not running nowhere."

Nazir was trying to lighten the dark mood, but when he saw it wasn't working, he became even more concerned.

"Please," I whispered, tears streaming down my face.

I couldn't tell him that my father was trying to force me to marry another man. It would be too painful to say those words to him. I just needed him to know I wanted to be with him.

"Tata, why you wanna leave?"

"I'm tired of trying to live up to my parents' standards and the expectations they set for me. I want something new. I want simple. Isn't that what you want, too, baby?"

He wiped the tears from my cheeks and gently kissed my lips. "Yes, Tata, but that's not the way to do this. It would hurt your parents."

"Please, baby," I pleaded. "I can make things right afterward. Right now, I just want to leave and figure out life somewhere else—get married."

I desperately wanted him to agree to run away with me. If I left with him, my father wouldn't be able to force me into marrying someone I didn't know or love.

He exhaled deeply. "I'm working on some things for us, baby. I want to give you that simple life, but I also don't want to tear your family apart in the process."

"Please." I kissed his lips and slowly removed the silk pajama top I was wearing.

His eyes took me in as he pushed me back onto the bed, hovering over me. He pressed his lips roughly against mine while sliding down my pajama shorts and pulling off his pants. I craved his body as much as he craved mine.

"I'm gonna fuck this pussy good," he growled near my ear. "Then you gonna fall asleep in my arms. We'll figure the rest of this shit out tomorrow."

"Yessss, Zir. Fuck me," I begged.

Every part of my body responded to him. His words were like strings, and my body moved with his every command. Pushing my legs apart, he shoved himself deep inside of me. I've been handled like fragile glass my entire life, so I welcomed his aggressiveness. Arching my back, I took all of him. Then he slowly pulled out before slamming inside me again as I whimpered. I needed this. It had been an emotional day, and my mind had been racing ever since I stepped into my condo after flying back. But whenever Nazir plugged me up, everything always went silent. The world seemed quieter, and it was just the two of us in that moment.

"Fuck, Tata. You know you my world, right?"

"I know, baby. I… I…" I moaned.

"Say what you mean and mean what you say, beloved," he grunted, reciting his favorite saying.

His strong, long strokes made me feel them in my eyelids, and I screamed in ecstasy.

Because my father bought the two empty condos on either side of mine, I didn't have to worry about anyone hearing my cries of passion. My wish was to turn this entire floor into my dream condo, and since I got everything I wanted, he planned to make that happen for me.

"Where your mind at, Tata? Tell me. You not feeling this dick in your guts? Tell a nigga something, baby," he grunted.

Raising my upper body from the bed, I started sucking on his lips. In response, he shoved his tongue down my throat and his dick up my vagina. I swear he was touching my intestines. It felt so good, his ass had me panting like a rabid dog. I was right there. The orgasm was slow-building, like ice cream churning inside a machine. Just as I was about to explode, he flipped me on my stomach, entered me from behind, and smacked my ass, causing it to ripple.

"Zir...God...please...I'm going to..." I moaned, rocking to meet his thrusts.

Sex between us was always so special. Nazir, who was usually gentle with me, turned into someone else. He treated me the way I wanted to be treated in the bedroom—never handling me with white gloves. Yes, we made love, and during our lovemaking, he would handle me as if I were the most precious jewel in the world. But when we fucked? He made sure to fuck me properly. And after the day I had with my father, I needed this more than he could have known.

With a firm grip on my hips, Nazir slammed me against him until I felt his body stiffen and his semen coat my walls. Then he collapsed beside me and pulled me on top of him, holding me tightly.

"I love you, Tata."

"I love you more, Zir," I said blissfully, then kissed his chest and closed my eyes, falling asleep to his scent that always brought me comfort.

CHAPTER ONE

Tatiana Sterling

TEN YEARS LATER...

THEY SAY DEATH repeats itself in an endless cycle because grief won't let you forget. I am living proof of that truth. Standing at my husband's grave, I felt the same sickness I felt two years ago.

Karim and I never got along. In fact, I hated him when we first met. He was arrogant, overly confident, and swore he was God's gift to the world. At first, I resented his existence, thinking that if he had never been born, I wouldn't have been forced to marry him. Despite my heartbreak, I had to push through and do what was best for the family's greater good.

College was my escape from my life in Greenwich, but after Nazir left me, it never felt the same. I didn't have time to drown in my feelings, though. No, I had a wedding to attend—my own wedding. I was *forced* to stand before God, exchanging vows with a man I didn't want or love. But God proved to me that I was a liar because here I was—standing at Karim's grave and mourning him on what would have been his 35th birthday. No candles.

No celebration. Only me left to pick up the broken pieces of our marriage.

I never thought I would fall in love with him. Our fathers wanted this union, not me, and I swore to myself I would never give Karim my heart. Honestly, my heart was already broken. So I figured, why not marry the rich man's son and go along with the plot for my life? But somewhere along the way, that plot twisted and turned into eight years of loving and respecting each other. And it ended with the doctor telling me he didn't make it. Now, I stood heartbroken, still asking the same question I had back then: *God, why take me through all of this only to leave me broken in the end?*

"Babes, you have lunch with your father at Miller's Pointe," Yaya, my assistant, reminded me as I stared at the onyx gravestone engraved with the words: *Son, husband, father, and friend until the end.*

Picking up a nearby rock, I brushed away some dirt from the headstone and placed it on top. All I could think about was all the wasted time during our first two years of marriage—those two years we spent hating everything about each other.

Shoving my hands into the pockets of my Mackage trench coat, I walked through the cemetery until I made it back to the black-tinted SUV my father had sent for me. Visiting Karim on his birthday was a priority for me, so I didn't care about making him wait.

Yaya quickly rounded the truck to her side as the driver held the door open for me to get in. As I settled into my seat, I pulled my vibrating phone out of my pocket. A smile spread across my face as I looked at the incoming FaceTime call.

"Hi, baby. How was school today?"

She smiled, mirroring my own expression. "It was cool, Mom. Um, how happy are you right now?"

I narrowed my eyes at my daughter as she sheepishly smiled, knowing she was about to tell me something that wouldn't make me happy. "Why, Nazira?"

She huffed into the phone. "I lost my lunchbox again," she said, then quickly added, "I promise I'm going to find it tomorrow."

This was her third lunchbox this school year. Every time she promised to find it, but she never did, because it was, in fact, lost. Nazira was a free-spirited child who reminded me of myself once upon a time. As much as she was a free spirit, she was also determined, diligent, and responsible. Well, she was responsible except when it came to keeping up with her lunchbox.

"Zira, you said that last time, and we had to buy another one. How does someone keep losing their lunchbox?"

She sighed loudly before running down the story of what happened *again*, being very theatrical because she was a theater kid. We used to see shows on Broadway at least once a month. After we lost Karim, we went more often to lift our spirits.

"...And that's how I lost my lunchbox."

"Nazira, I'm starting to think you're losing them on purpose because you want to eat the school lunches instead of the ones I pack for you."

I caught a spark of mischief in her eyes.

"Not true, Mom. When are you coming home?" she asked, quickly changing the subject.

Her school had an early dismissal today, which meant she was home sooner than expected. Bloom, her au pair, usually picked her up when I couldn't, and since I was meeting with my father, today was one of those days.

"I have lunch with your grandfather. Once I'm finished, I'll be home."

Nazira perked up. "Can we stay in the city and catch a Broadway show? It's the weekend, and I don't have school on Monday."

The last two years had been hard for us both emotionally. I no longer felt like myself, as though part of me was missing.

Karim.

He was supposed to be here beside me, but he was gone. As a mother, I did my best to be present and help my daughter carry her grief while carrying my own. I had lost a husband, and she had lost a father. Neither pain outweighed the other, and once I realized that and checked myself, things became less foggy. Therapy twice a week, along with lots of quality time, helped us. Work consumed much of my time, but I appreciated the distraction from feeling lonely. I never thought I'd get to the point where I would want to discover love again, but there were days when I craved love and someone's touch.

"Mom? Hello?"

"Sorry, baby. I'll have Yaya look up some shows, and then we'll head to the city once I'm done."

"Already on it," Yaya whispered, holding up her phone.

Nazira cheered. "Thanks, Mom. You're the best. Love you, stinky socks."

I chuckled. "Love you more, rotten cheese."

We had been saying that since she was five years old, and I hoped we would continue saying it until she had children of her own and could pass it down to them.

After ending the FaceTime call with Nazira, I leaned my head back against the seat as the driver took us to my father's favorite restaurant—a place where he always held meetings and where the staff treated him like royalty.

Miller's Pointe sat right by the water, offering views of boats docking and fishermen unloading their catches of the day. I loved the food there, but it wasn't my favorite spot. I mostly ate there when I wanted to feel pampered because I was Malcolm Rich's daughter. Those people would spoon-feed me if I asked. That's how much they loved and respected my family in Greenwich Pointe. The Rich and Sterling families practically ruled this city, and it made me sick. I refused to raise my daughter to feel entitled like some of my in-laws and my own family did. They walked around with a sense of entitlement, as if the entire world owed them something.

"Although she's seen it many times, I managed to snag *Hamilton* tickets," Yaya said, distracting me from my thoughts.

"Do you think she remembers today is his birthday?"

Yaya put her phone down and rested her hand on top of mine. "Maybe. It's also your responsibility to remind her, Tatiana. I know you don't want to upset her, but she deserves to celebrate her father, even if he's no longer here."

"You're right," I sighed.

Talking about Karim with Nazira was hard because I didn't want to make her sad. I was the one who held her all night after he passed away. The next morning, she came downstairs asking for her father even though she knew he was gone. A small piece of my little girl died when her father left us, so I was always careful about how I brought up Karim. The joy was returning to her, and I never wanted to see it disappear. I would be miserable forever if that meant my baby could stay happy.

"I also need you to stop pretending like he didn't exist with Nazira. The two of you should be celebrating him together on birthdays and holidays." Yaya squeezed my hand.

"Thanks, Ya."

Yalina and Liliana—whom we called Bloom—were my best friends, and I also hired them to help manage my busy life. Yaya was organized and detail-oriented, while Bloom was loving and nurturing. So, it only made sense to hire Yaya as my assistant and Bloom as my nanny.

After getting married, I remember sitting on a reformer in a Pilates studio in town, feeling sick to my stomach and heartbroken. Yaya had finished her workout, and her sister was sitting on another reformer. They watched as I counted down in my head, overwhelmed with regret. When I suddenly stood up and bolted to the bathroom, they followed.

Two strangers held my hair as I vomited into the toilet. They stayed right there with me, offering a wet napkin and water as I dry heaved.

I learned they weren't from Greenwich Pointe but from the next town over. Yaya and Bloom didn't come from wealthy families; they worked at a nearby strip club. They were hood twins—same father, different mothers—and their father was strict about them knowing each other and having a relationship. Despite our different backgrounds, we became inseparable from that moment on.

No matter how I felt about marrying Karim, the vomiting that day was a sign from Nazira that she existed, and we would be welcoming her into our lives.

"Please don't let him get under your skin, Tati," Yaya warned as we pulled up in front of the restaurant.

I've never been a daddy's girl, and it's a topic my therapist and I often discussed during my sessions. While Nazira loved everything about Karim and would be inside his skin if she could when he was alive, I felt completely the opposite about my father.

"Why does he want to meet with me anyway?" I asked, even though I knew Yaya didn't have the answer.

I refused to believe this was just a casual lunch to "catch up". Malcolm Rich didn't do casual. If he was reaching out, it was because there was something in it for him. Honestly, I didn't have the energy to deal with him—especially not today. Today was already heavy enough. It was my late husband's birthday, and I still needed to check in on my mother-in-law. She'd lost her son two years ago, and just last month, she buried her husband.

Raphael Sterling was quiet, stoic, and a man of few words—but his love for his family ran deep. He showed me the fatherly affection I'd been missing all my life.

Placing a hand on my chest, I sighed. I could still hear his deep laugh and feel the way he would pull me into a hug, kissing both my cheeks before teasingly asking, *"Bella, are you alright? My son has given you the world, hmm?"*

Raphael Sterling was Black, and Carlotta was Italian. Despite being Black, he spoke fluent Italian with his wife. The Sterlings only had one child, Karim, but they had always hoped to give him a sister. That wish never came true—until I married into the family. Raphael cherished me as if I were his own flesh and blood. To him, I was the daughter he never had.

The driver opened the door, and I grabbed my purse from the seat before exiting and walking around the truck. Yaya was right beside me as we entered the restaurant. I didn't need to give my name because the staff recognized me immediately.

"Mrs. Sterling, how are you this afternoon?" the hostess asked nervously, which probably meant my father was somewhere inside acting like a tyrant.

I smiled. "Hi, Lucy. I'm doing great. How are you and the baby?"

Unlike my father, I enjoyed connecting with the people who worked and served me. I picked up this trait from Raphael, who treated everyone with the same respect—whether it was a janitor or the CEO of a corporation. In his eyes, respect was respect. It didn't matter what position you held.

She quickly pulled out her phone and showed me a picture of the adorable blue-eyed baby.

"She's three months old now and can hold her head up. I asked the doctor if that was normal," she rambled on, proud of her creation.

"Nazira started holding her head up around the same age. These babies are more advanced than we were. She's beautiful, Lucy."

"Thank you, and thank you so much for the stroller. I really appreciate it, Mrs. Sterling."

"Tatiana," I replied, touching her arm. "I think I can find my father. I know he has to be seated near the largest window."

She nodded. "Let me know if you need anything."

I watched as she quickly put her phone down and went to greet the next patron. Yaya and I proceeded further into the restaurant, and as expected, I spotted my father sitting at a table near the biggest bay window, with a perfect view of the small harbor.

His head was down and his brows were furrowed as he looked at his phone, like he had received bad news through an email or text. I cleared my throat, and that's when he finally looked up. Malcolm Rich was fifty-six but didn't look a day over forty. He had a rich brown complexion, salt-and-pepper beard, light brown, hardened eyes, and a forehead that some might mistake for laugh lines, but they were lines from scowling—never wearing a smile, always stressed about something he couldn't control.

"Tatiana." He stood, greeted me with a kiss on the cheek, and gave me a tight hug before letting go.

"How are you, Yaya?" he asked, smiling at her before pulling out both of our chairs.

"Doing great, Mr. Rich," she replied as we settled into our seats. "Can't complain. And you?"

He chuckled while lowering himself into his chair. "Ah, I'd like to complain, but I can't. Getting old is no excuse."

She laughed and immediately began scanning the menu. My eyes caught my father as he used a napkin to wipe his forehead before picking up his drink. When he noticed me watching, he smiled and leaned back.

"How's my granddaughter?" he asked.

I unfolded the cloth napkin and placed it across my lap. "She's doing great—smart, beautiful, and dare I say dramatic, too. Maybe you should visit her more. Mom isn't always around."

He sucked his teeth and looked away. "Business has been demanding. You don't think I'd rather spend my time watching my only grandchild grow?"

"Business that you can pay anyone to handle, Daddy," I shot back. "I'll never understand your obsession with money. We're more than blessed, but you always want more."

Karim always spoke about how my father and greed went together in the same sentence. Nothing ever satisfied Malcolm. The homes, the villas in other countries, the jets, and the cars—none of it was enough. He always desired more.

He threw back the rest of his drink and looked at me with those piercing eyes. "With the alimony I'm currently paying your mother, I'll be working until I'm even older and grayer."

I narrowed my eyes at him. "Is it really about Mom—or the fact that your new girlfriend is only a year younger than me?"

Children usually struggle with accepting their parents' divorce, but not me. A year after Karim's death, my mother told me that she was divorcing my father. She wasn't happy and refused to stay miserable with a man who refused to change. Waiting for Malcolm Rich to change was like expecting the Statue of Liberty to be moved to Mexico—it would never happen. She grew tired of waiting for him to make her happy and love her like he promised. Even though it was an arranged marriage, I believe my mother fell in love with my father over time, just as I fell in love with Karim.

She married my father, gave birth to his child, and made sure I was raised with lots of love. She dedicated her life to being there whenever he needed her. In return, she was left feeling lonely, unappreciated, and irrelevant. My mother was never a priority, so I was glad when she finally chose herself and left him.

Not even six months after their divorce, my father popped out with a younger woman, leading me to believe she had always been around. Now that he was no longer married to my mother, he could bring her out of the shadows. He needed someone on his arm, and she filled that role just like my mother once did. I don't know if he intended to marry her. All I knew was that he started referring to her as the future Mrs. Rich. For all I knew, he might have already stupidly married her.

He snapped his fingers rudely, signaling for the server to bring him another drink. "Portia has nothing to do with what your mother and I have going on. Has she mentioned her new boyfriend to you? Heard he's into stocks and has a ton of money. What the hell does she need mine for?"

"Yes, she's told me about Wyatt. I actually like him." I smiled, genuinely happy that my mother was finally being loved the right way. "But how do you know about him? She's been very discreet with their relationship."

He waved me off, knowing that I knew he had his ways of prying into my mother's life. Men could be so weird. When he had her, he never poured back into her as her husband. Hell, he barely acknowledged her. Now that she had finally chosen herself and walked away, he suddenly wanted to keep tabs on her.

"I wanted to meet with you to discuss our families and the businesses we have together. With Raphacl gone, everything falls on your shoulders, Tatiana. Carlotta's no help because when I spoke to her, all she did was give me her lawyer's number."

"She just lost her husband, Dad. Why would you expect her to discuss business right now?"

He looked at me as he polished off his second drink. "Because business doesn't stop when someone dies. Death is part of life, and we have to learn how to navigate it and keep going."

I stared at him in shock. I could tell by Yaya's expression that she was also taken aback by his cold response.

Carlotta and Raphael had been married for years before Karim was even conceived. Until his last days, the love they shared was loud and bright. It was one of the things I admired most about Karim and his parents. He had been raised in love—a love so powerful that it enveloped you as soon as you entered their home. I knew what love felt like from my mother. But with my father, I always felt like I was just an accomplishment on his to-do list, never experiencing that familiar feeling of being a daddy's girl or being able to run to him when I needed something. He wasn't my first love or my first hero.

Nazir was.

As I sat across from him on my late husband's birthday and after losing my father-in-law not too long ago, he showed no concern other than the business he wanted to discuss. It was foolish of me to think he invited me to lunch to ask how I was holding up or how I was managing to be the strength for the family that he forced me to marry into.

"I spoke with our family's lawyer, and we have a meeting soon to go over things. The family is mourning right now, and we shouldn't be worrying about business when we've lost someone we loved so much."

"He was—" my father blurted, then composed himself, straightening his suit jacket and glancing at Yaya, who was focused on the menu. "Raphael is no longer here, and he isn't coming back. That's the reality. You and Carlotta aren't equipped to handle the magnitude of business that Raphael managed daily."

"Dad, he was your friend. Don't you feel anything about his passing? Is business all you care about?"

I could tell he was getting frustrated because he was being put on the spot. Malcolm Rich was the one who put others on the spot, not the other way around.

"Tati, I lost a very close friend, but the only way I know how to cope with my grief is by working through it. Before Raph passed, he told me he wanted me to take control of everything so you never had to worry."

Neither Carlotta nor I had the strength to watch the video Raphael left behind, a recording he made shortly after Nazira's birth to update everything. I knew I had to be the one to view it and meet with the lawyers. It was difficult bearing all this weight, especially with my father acting like a rabid dog, biting at my ankles to help.

"I will let you know when I need your help, Daddy. Right now, I just need you here as a father. When I meet with the lawyer, I will tell you if there is something for you to do."

He was focused on trying to help me, even though I never asked for it. I understood that this was my father's way of offering support and comfort as I mourned. Business was his forte, and he believed his help could ease some of my stress. It was his version of giving a hug to comfort his grieving daughter.

Raphael had been sick for several years, so we all knew his death was coming. Karim's sudden and unexpected passing, however, left me in a fog of grief for a while. Now that I was working through it, my father wanted to be there. But where was he when I was clutching Karim's T-shirt in the walk-in closet, crying until I could hardly catch my breath, or the days I struggled to get out of bed to care for my daughter? He wasn't there then, but now he wanted to step in.

Bullshit.

With his attention on his phone, he replied, "Tatiana, my job has always been to protect you, but you're making it very hard for me to do that."

I watched as he silenced it and then looked back up at me.

"I'm not trying to make it hard. Raphael also prepared both me and Karim for what would come next if he passed."

"Well, now they are both gone, and the Sterling name is barely hanging on," he scoffed, glancing at his ringing phone again. The more he ignored the call, the more irritated he seemed to get. "Nazira isn't going to carry on the name, considering she's not biologically a Sterling."

"Wow," Yaya muttered, clearly disgusted by his words.

I fought to keep my composure. "What do you mean?"

The only people who knew that Nazira wasn't Karim's biological daughter were Karim, his parents, Yaya, Bloom, and my mother. I never bothered telling my father because, as long as I married into the Sterling family, I knew he wouldn't care.

Once again, he casually waved me off and took a sip of his water. "Please, Tatiana. I already knew Nazira wasn't Karim's daughter. You didn't let that man breathe in your direction, and you expect me to believe he impregnated you? You were pregnant when you got married. Thank God your being a slut didn't ruin the deal I had put in place."

Leaning back, he lit a cigarette and took a long drag while staring at me. My words caught in my throat as I looked at him. The nerve of him to say those things when he auctioned me off like prime stock at a market.

"How dare you speak on something you never cared about until money came into the equation," I snapped. "The only reason I'm even here is because you want control of the Sterling empire. You don't give a damn about anything I've been going through."

"Clearly you haven't missed a meal, Tati," he shot back, smoke curling from his lips.

"Oh, hell no," Yaya said sharply, jumping up from her chair.

My father turned to face her, appearing calm and unfazed that she was eyeing the steak knife only inches from her hand.

"Look, I have more important things that need my attention than wasting my time having a conversation with an immature man who lost his family."

I stood up as my father put out his cigarette. He then raised the hand holding the unlit cigarette to his temple and peered up at me.

"Shit, Tati...I apologize. Things have been stressful, and I'm just trying to keep everything together."

"By attacking my weight? Dad, I have everything under control on my end. If I need any help, I'll let you or Walter know."

"Walt? Why the hell would you let him know anything? He's not even your blood relative."

Walter was my godfather and more of a father to me than my own. I used to call them best friends, but over the years, I noticed how Walt started to distance himself from my father.

When I was growing up, he and his wife moved to Greenwich Pointe to be closer to me. Walt and Aja were involved in everything–whether it was my sports games, recitals, or other events. They cheered with my mother from the bleachers and made sure to attend every performance, even if they had to rush across town.

"That man has been there through everything in my life. I don't care that he's not blood-related. He's my family."

"Heard you have Nazira calling him Pop-Pop," He shook his head, flicking the cigarette into the dish in front of him.

Nazira knew Walt better than my own father. My father would visit whenever the mood struck him, which wasn't often. With children, you have to be consistent, and my father wasn't, just like he hadn't been for me. Walt, on the other hand, was very involved in my daughter's life. He and Aja never had children of their own, so Nazira was their whole world. I was grateful to have so much support in raising my daughter.

"He's just as much her grandfather as you are. Maybe you should come around more often instead of criticizing her mother's weight. By the way, I have no problem with my weight. I'm perfectly healthy, and my husband had no issues with it either. Have a great day, Father."

"The husband I had to set your ass up with in the first place," he hollered behind me.

I tightly clutched my purse as I left the restaurant with Yaya behind me. I knew she regretted not poking him in the throat with that steak knife. If she didn't, I sure as hell did.

CHAPTER TWO

Tatiana

PAST: A FEW WEEKS AFTER THE WEDDING...

"**WHEN WERE YOU** going to tell me that you're pregnant?"

Karim's voice sent a chill down my spine as I gripped the handle of the fridge.

It was a little past midnight, and sleep was hard to find. I tossed and turned while flashes of Nazir flooded my mind. One minute I was hot, then I was cold, and in the end, all I wanted was to be in Nazir's arms—not living with a man I never wanted to marry.

Karim leaned against the counter with his arms crossed over his chest. He was wearing a pair of grey pajama pants and no shirt, waiting for me to speak.

It should have been illegal to be as rich and handsome as he was. His light brown skin, sharp jawline, full lips, and curly low fade were enough to make any woman swoon. He reminded me so much of the actor Keith Powers. If Keith Powers didn't know he had a twin, well, he had one, and he lived in a gorgeous twenty-thousand-square-foot mansion in Greenwich Pointe.

Yes, Karim was attractive, but he wasn't Nazir. No one could make me feel the way Nazir did, and for him to leave me without a warning, an explanation, or even a note shattered my heart. It became even more painful for me after seeing the positive pregnancy test. I was carrying his child, but I was married to another man.

I could no longer hide the truth from Karim. Even though he was always working and rarely home, he couldn't miss that something was wrong with me. I was sick all the time, and every time I saw myself in the mirror, I looked like I had been fighting my whole life and the fight was winning.

"You know I had to walk away from the love of my life, too, Tatiana. Shit isn't just about you. You're not the only one who had to make sacrifices for this family."

I looked down at my feet. "Why was it so important for us to get married? I was happy in college, living my own life. I never wanted any of this."

He uncrossed his arms and slipped his hands into his pajama pockets. "I had made a home in Miami and didn't want to come back here either. But as the only children of our parents, some things were already in place before we could even crawl. So, this is our reality."

"I can't get rid of my baby. It's the only thing..."

My voice cracked, unable to finish. Thoughts of Nazir were too painful.

Karim nodded. "I would never ask you to. We're married, so that means the baby will be a Sterling. Nobody needs to know she's not biologically mine."

I looked into his soft eyes. "You would do that for me?"

"Yeah."

I smiled at him. "I've been a jerk to you."

"Hell yeah. Finishing the last of the orange juice is wild."

He chuckled, and I snorted.

"I'm so angry, hurt, and sad. I took everything out on you, and I apologize for that. But my question is, why aren't you feeling the same?"

"I've always been taught to roll with the punches, so that's what I do. Ever since I entered the world as Raphael Sterling's only heir, my life hasn't truly been my own. If my father has a plan for me, I trust he means well and would never lead me astray."

"Can't say the same for my father."

He stepped away from the counter and came closer, towering over me as he looked into my eyes.

"Tati, we can either hate each other or get to know one another and make the most of this marriage. The choice is yours."

I met his light brown eyes and gave a faint smile. "What do we tell our parents about my baby?"

He gently touched my cheek and then kissed it. "Our baby."

CHAPTER THREE

Tatiana

I ALWAYS SLEPT best in the city. The car horns, random shouting, and distant sirens acted as my personal sound machine. Sleep would come to me like an infant after eating baby cereal and drinking a bottle of formula. At our Greenwich home, things were different. I would try almost anything to fall asleep, but nothing seemed to work. When I pulled back the covers and got into bed, I'd lie there staring at the ceiling while counting backwards from a million. It was hard to get a good night's sleep in a home that once overflowed with love.

Yet, despite how our story began, it grew into something beautiful. Karim was patient, kind, and loving—the same qualities I missed with Nazir. We showed each other grace because neither of us was perfect. Raised by a father who solved all of his mother's problems, Karim naturally became a man who tried to do the same, remaining by my side despite the baggage I carried.

For the first two months after we got married, I stayed at my condo in the city and only went home when he texted me that his parents or mine were coming over for lunch or dinner. Karim was understanding that way. He knew I needed my space and time to process everything happening. It was never about him, but more about me. I was fighting with myself not to love this man. My first true love had abandoned me, and I didn't want to be vulnerable with anyone else like that again.

After silencing my annoying alarm, I sat up in bed and admired the city skyline and skyscrapers. The breathtaking view made me wake up feeling refreshed and excited for the day.

Sliding the silk sheet off my body, I swung my legs over the bed's edge and stretched before placing my feet on the wooden floor. I looked back at my bed and decided I would make it after finishing my morning routine. Before heading downstairs to the gym, I quietly tiptoed down the hall to check on Nazira, who was still sleeping soundly. Despite having a queen-sized bed to herself, she still took up the entire bed, with her legs and arms sprawled across the mattress.

Smiling, I gently closed her door and then went to the bathroom to brush my teeth and wash my face. I would wait until after my workout to do my skincare routine and take a shower.

As I slipped out of my pajamas, I looked at my size-eighteen reflection in the mirror and smiled. I gave my booty a little bounce, admiring the body that had given me my angel down the hall. I've always been curvy, and my mother raised me to appreciate the body God blessed me with. I never went through that phase of wanting to be skinny to fit in. My mother built my confidence throughout my childhood, which is why I wasn't offended when my father made that smart remark. The comment might have offended someone insecure about her body, but not me. I was very confident and knew I was that bitch.

Ever since I was a kid, I've been passionate about fitness. I played softball, soccer, and even tried running track until I realized it wasn't for me. I've always been active and loved doing anything physical, especially to avoid gaining too much weight.

My daughter was the complete opposite. Nazira inherited my mother's genes and was naturally thin. The girl had the appetite of a football player but never gained weight. I envied her metabolism.

I put on my sports bra with matching leggings and then went to the kitchen to grab my favorite water bottle, iPad Mini, and earbuds. Given my busy schedule, I made working out in the morning a priority; it helped me get the energy I needed to get through my hectic days.

Nazira knew my routine, so I usually found her eating breakfast with her iPad propped up whenever she woke up before I returned. I was truly blessed to have a child who was so easygoing and independent. Besides her constant habit of losing her lunchbox, she never gave me any trouble.

She reminded me a lot of myself, and sometimes I felt guilty about it. Growing up as an only child, I was forced to be independent and resourceful, and I had to mature faster than my friends. I often overheard adult conversations around me, and sometimes I was even included in those conversations. Nazira was very mature for her age, and at times, I had to remind myself that she's only ten. Even though I liked to call her my little bestie, I had to remember she was still a child, and I couldn't vent to her the way my mother did with me at her age.

As a child, I knew too much because my mother treated me like her personal diary, sharing things I shouldn't have known. I never blamed her and was always there for her, understanding her loneliness. However, I chose to raise my daughter differently, refusing to make her feel older than she was. I wanted her to enjoy being a child for as long as possible and kept my loneliness and sadness hidden from her as best I could.

I used my key fob to enter the state-of-the-art gym. With my iPad on the treadmill and earbuds in, I stretched before starting the machine. Just as I was about to hit play on my favorite workout playlist, Yaya's name popped up on my phone's screen.

"Yes, Yalina," I answered with a sigh.

She snorted. "Well, you can at least pretend to be excited to hear from me."

"Calling at this hour and expecting me to be excited is actually nuts. I'm more anxious about why you're calling me."

Yaya laughed. "No bad news. The location you wanted for the spa's second site is available, and the realtor says we can sign the papers whenever you're ready."

I did a little jump while still maintaining my stride on the treadmill, excited because the location I'd wanted was perfect.

"Have him send the documents over electronically. I want to secure this location quickly."

I could hear Yalina typing rapidly on the other end.

"Drafting his email now. Have you spoken to your mother about you and Zira possibly moving to the city?"

This time, I snorted. "Nope."

"Girl, you said you would. How do you think moving her only grandchild away without telling her will make her feel?"

"Yaya, we're not relocating across the country. I haven't even discussed it with Carlotta yet. Excuse me for wanting to finalize everything before bringing it up to them."

Nazira was everyone's favorite, and everyone wanted time with her. If she wasn't at my mother's house, she was at Carlotta's or Walt and Aja's. So, I knew they wouldn't be happy about that news.

"You'd better. Anyway, did Bloom go with you to the city?"

"She flew with us but said she had her own plans. When we're in the city, I don't need her to help me with Zira. Why? Is everything okay?"

"My father called and said he heard she was messing with that man again. And you know how Bloom is. She'll get defensive if I meddle in her business."

"And you think she won't with me?" I asked. "She's made it clear that our work and personal lives are separate, Yalina. She's grown. We can't keep babying her."

Yaya sighed. "I don't want to baby her. I just don't want to see her waste her life on that nigga again. After the way things ended, I thought she'd finally be done with him."

Although we were all thick as thieves, Bloom kept her love life private. We only knew what she chose to share. What I did know was her ex was the reason she once showed up at my front door with her eyes swollen and red from crying and a suitcase in hand.

That man dragged her through hell, and she mistook it for heaven. She thought that because he claimed to love her, the pain and chaos he caused somehow proved it was real love. I told her many times that love doesn't feel like hell. Love feels like curling up on the couch and watching your favorite comfort movie during a thunderstorm. Sure, the thunder might startle you, but instead of fear, it just sets the perfect background for a relaxing evening. It's loud, wild, and unpredictable, but never unbearable. That's what love felt like to me. I constantly reminded Bloom that just because a man says he loves you doesn't mean he truly does. As her sister, Yaya wanted to protect her. She could see as clear as day that Bloom's boyfriend was no good and wanted to shield her from what she knew was coming. But Bloom wanted to live life on her own terms. Her choices were hers to make, even if that meant stumbling.

"She's stubborn," I said softly. "You can't control her life. She has to make her own mistakes. Hopefully, this last spin the block will finally show her he's not the right man."

"Yeah," Yaya sighed. "Hopefully."

"I love you, Yaya," I said with a smile, keeping pace on the treadmill.

"Love you, too. Oh, don't forget we have that meeting with the skincare company. Also, Jonah wants to discuss opening a location in the Dominican Republic at that new resort."

I groaned. "He's corrupted you, too?"

Yaya chuckled. "He may have called and asked me to add the meeting to your calendar."

"He wants to expand too quickly, and I don't think I'm ready for that." I increased the incline and wiped the sweat from my brow.

"Tatiana, you've had Hush for six years. It's the most sought-after spa in the area. People travel from the city to Greenwich just to visit. It's time to stop being scared and expand."

"I worry about Nazira. Expanding means I'll spend more time away from her, traveling and fulfilling other commitments. I don't think she's ready for that."

"Is she not ready, or are you not ready? You have a support system that will gladly step in and make sure Nazira is cared for. Plus, you pay Bloom good money to do that. I think you're making excuses."

"Well, I think you and Jonah like each other, and you're making excuses to see him."

Yaya laughed. "And I think you just want me to move on and are trying to push Jonah into my arms."

"Is a girl wrong for trying? You deserve the world, Yalina. Jonah could give it to you."

As usual, she ignored me and went right back to business.

"Listen, you have the support, and every investor wants a piece of what you've built. The city location is going to be huge, so it only makes sense to keep expanding. And stop turning down interviews. Do those, as well—but baby steps."

"I'm going to kill both you and Jonah," I muttered.

"Yeah, well, you'll have to come to the meeting to do that. See you in a few hours—and kiss Zira for me."

"Whatever," I smirked and ended the call.

Hush was my second child. After endless conversations with Karim about having another baby, I realized he wasn't going to change his mind, and I needed something to channel my energy into. My mom came over one afternoon, talking about how one of her friends was selling her spa and moving out of the country. She went on and on about how it was the only black-owned spa in the area and how she hated going to the other spas because no one ever treated her skin properly. I listened to her for weeks before finally deciding to visit the spa. The moment I stepped inside, I knew. My body relaxed as the scent of santal drifted through the air. I've always been into skincare and self-care. My mother had been taking me to spas since I was seven, teaching me early the importance of pouring back into yourself.

When my treatments ended, I met the owner, and what started as a quick introduction turned into us chatting in her office like old friends while sipping champagne. She shared her dreams of traveling, which she had put on hold to raise her children, and how she had missed out on love twice because she had chosen her career instead. She spoke with so much wisdom, being transparent about her sacrifices and regrets.

I used to have a plan for my life too, but when I got married, that plan crumbled. I had gone from wanting an exciting life in New York City to living in the suburbs with a husband and a child. Before becoming Tatiana Sterling, I wanted to be someone––a woman with her own plan and her own money. I had been kept my entire life, and I swore I'd never become a kept woman.

We talked until closing time, and that's when I offered to buy her spa. She laughed, thinking I was joking, until I pulled out my checkbook and asked her number. It took her a moment to realize I was serious, but once she did, she told me the amount, and I wrote the check without hesitation. The next week, I shadowed her at the spa and learned everything I needed to know. We signed the papers, and she hugged me with tears in her eyes. Her dream had come true—she was able to sell her home and travel the world.

While Jennifer was ending her chapter as a spa owner, I was starting mine. I rebranded everything, from the name to the interior, added new treatments, and hired the best of the best. Besides loving being a mother to my baby, this was what excited me and motivated me to get out of bed each morning.

Like always, Karim was right there to offer advice and support. Raphael covered the entire cost of renovating the space and even bought the wellness store next door to expand the spa. My mother was excited that a Black-owned spa would stay in Greenwich, and everyone was happy about it. Except my father. He didn't understand why I was starting a business when I had a husband. Malcolm couldn't understand why Karim was so supportive of his wife having something of her own.

Hush Spa was opened, and our clientele doubled overnight. We were the most talked-about spa in Greenwich, and we still are. Expansion was something Karim and I discussed before he passed away, but after his death, I shut down all talk of that. Growing something we built together without him didn't feel right.

Jonah—Karim's best friend and Nazira's godfather—was also an investor in Hush. Since the day we lowered Karim into the ground, he had been there for me. I could count on him to show up with takeout because he knew I didn't cook, or to send a random text just to check in. Throughout this grieving process, I honestly don't think I could have managed any of this without my family, my girls, and Jonah.

My phone chimed, breaking my thoughts.

Jonah: *What did the fucking chicken say to the duck?*

I chuckled at his text message.

Me: *What?*

Jonah: *Answer the fucking phone and take it off DND.*

Jonah: *The Valora wants to talk about opening a Hush location in their Vegas resort.*

I chuckled again, closing the screen to focus on the rest of my workout—though my nerves were getting the best of me. Maybe this was the next chapter God was pushing me toward, whether I was ready or not.

CHAPTER FOUR

Yalina "Yaya" Blackwell

"DAMN, YA. YOU not even listening. Fuck," Sav barked into the phone.

I stared at my phone sitting on the counter on speaker, rolling my eyes as I turned my attention back to my laptop.

"Sorry. I was reading this email before my next meeting."

"Always about fucking work whenever I'm on the phone," she continued.

I nearly popped my eyeballs out of my sockets from how hard I rolled them before powering off my laptop. Taking a deep breath, I counted down from ten before responding.

"Sav, I don't know why you think work stops because you called me. I can do both at the same time if you didn't know."

"Obviously, you can't if you didn't hear what the fuck I just said."

"What did you say?"

She paused.

I glanced at my watch, packed my laptop into my tote, grabbed an energy drink from the fridge, and slung my bag over my shoulder, holding the can in one hand and my phone in the other.

"Jonah came to visit me the other day—said he wanted to make sure I was straight."

This wasn't new news; Jonah had texted me beforehand to let me know he was going to visit her, which is why he missed our virtual meeting with the realtor.

"How'd it go?"

Even without me being in front of her, I could picture her shrugging.

"Shit was regular. He asked if I needed anything, and we talked for a little while. It felt strange seeing him in a suit and acting all proper, like he's not… never mind."

I snorted because Jonah was anything but proper. The only reason he probably wore a suit when he went to visit her was because he was going to or coming from a meeting. Jonah is very much the opposite of proper. I've lost count of how many times I had to pinch or elbow him during meetings because he would say whatever came to his mind without thinking first.

"He doesn't act proper. I mean, he wears a suit sometimes, but Jonah is definitely not proper," I said, biting the corner of my lip as I thought about Jonah Cross.

The line went quiet for a few seconds.

"Why the fuck do you know so much about how he acts, Yalina?"

I rolled my eyes and pressed the elevator button to go down to the parking garage, hoping my signal would weaken so I could end the call.

"He's Nazira's godfather. He's always around, Sav. Why do you act like I shouldn't know him?"

Sav was extremely jealous, and her jealousy worsened after she was arrested and sent upstate to serve time for a gun charge. I couldn't do anything without her becoming insanely jealous, which often led her to want to fight anyone she thought was even remotely interested in me. It's a miracle my friendship with Tatiana lasted because ever since Sav came into my life, she had a habit of pushing away anyone close to me. This was the reason Tatiana and Sav didn't get along, as well as why my relationship with my sister was strained. Sav had come between me and Bloom, creating a tension neither of us knew how to fix. We were trying, but the damage was already done.

Bloom hated Sav's possessiveness and disrespect. It was always about Sav, as if I wasn't on the outside holding down everything while she made pointless calls and always asked for money on her books. I could have tolerated it if she had left money behind. But it was my money supporting us, and all I ever got were complaints because I didn't do things quickly enough for her. Or if work consumed me and I was too exhausted to visit her, I was called selfish and unreliable. It was always about Sav's wants and needs, never about me.

We had been together for four years, with her incarcerated for two of those years. Our relationship was already rocky before Sav got locked up, and I had planned to end things because two years was enough wasted time. I was ready to move on and start a new chapter. But then Karim passed away, and I found myself torn between being there for my best friend and caring for my girlfriend, who had little family since her mother threw her out when she came out of the closet. I've always been a sucker and naïve when it comes to my heart. I kept people around who I should have cut off, and Sav was one of them. I let her manipulate my guilt, which resulted in us staying together, and me counting down until she was free so I could finally end it.

Sav worked for Karim, and I first met her when she came by the house to pick something up. Things were always kept quiet whenever it came to Karim's activities. Tatiana knew her family was involved in illegal dealings, but turned a blind eye. Whenever someone showed up, they would head straight down to his office to handle business.

I'd never thought about being with a woman—ever. I'd always been drawn to men, and no woman had ever caught my attention—until Sav. The day Sav walked in, my body reacted in a way it never had before. Her locs were twisted into long ropes that hung down her back, and tattoos covered every inch of her light skin. The one that hooked me was the tattoo of Lauryn Hill's iconic album cover. That album was everything to me, and seeing it etched into her skin had me intrigued. When she winked before swaggering behind Karim to his office, I couldn't look away.

But I wasn't gay...or was I?

At that time, Jonah lived in Miami and only visited the city for business or to spend time with Nazira. Sav, however, was always around because she was one of Karim's top workers. After Karim passed away, Jonah moved back to New York to be there for Tatiana and Nazira. He had been a silent investor in the spa, but recognizing that Tatiana was overwhelmed following Karim's death, he stepped up and took control to ensure Hush remained successful.

The only reason Jonah cared to visit Sav was out of respect for her relationship with Karim. He knew his best friend, and he thought Karim would have wanted to make sure she was good while serving her time. Jonah had always been loud with his dislike for Sav, saying she walked around like she had two balls in her pants instead of a pussy. She had a problem with respecting the pecking order, which is why they butted heads. With Karim now gone, where would that leave Sav? How would she make money? I knew Sav well, and I knew she would rather be homeless and broke than beg Jonah to work for him.

"If I was right in front of you, I'd put your head through the fucking wall again," Sav snarled into the phone.

I stared at my phone as if it were possessed.

"Then you'll end up in the emergency room with a knife sticking out of your leg…again," I responded, reminding her of what happened the last time she put her hands on me.

I would be damned if I allowed anyone to abuse me physically —especially a woman.

She chuckled. "Feisty ass. I told you I was sorry about that. You never apologized to me, though."

"I'm never going to apologize for defending myself. And for you to think that kind of violence is cute or something to joke about is sick." Reaching my car, I pressed the key fob to unlock the door. "Sav, I have to head to this meeting. Is that all you wanted?"

I was over the conversation before it even started. She never called to check on me or ask if I was okay. It was always about her, and I was drained. I wanted a relationship where someone genuinely cared about my feelings, would surprise me with flowers just because, and made me feel special on random days for no other reason than they valued me. I dreamed of that kind of love. But all I had was an aggressive bitch who acted like she was on her period all the time.

She sucked in her breath. I knew she wanted to say more but decided it would be best to stay quiet to avoid an argument.

"Nah," she replied.

"Cool," I said, quickly ending the call as I slid behind the steering wheel.

Before Sav went to prison, I felt lonely in our relationship and wasn't sure why I was holding on. I mean, I knew why, but did her happiness matter more than mine? I used to think that distance proved love was strong, but being apart taught me a great deal about myself. I've always struggled with understanding my sexuality since being with her. Each time I tried to have a conversation about it with Sav, she'd dismiss me, saying, "You like pussy, Yaya. I be sucking that shit off the bone, and you like it." What she didn't know was that I envisioned a man during our intimate moments. Sav used to get upset because I always wanted her to use a strap-on, and I never gave her oral sex. Then there was the time Bloom took me to a gay club for my birthday. I spent the entire time holding my drink and not interacting with anyone. This confusion about my sexuality lingered until Sav was gone. That's when I realized I wasn't gay. Yes, I loved Sav...but not women, if that makes sense.

Ending things with her wasn't just about my sexuality. It was about being tired of putting energy into a relationship that wasn't going anywhere. I was thirty-one, ready to have children and be someone's wife, which I had wanted since my twenties. With her, there were endless excuses when I brought up visiting fertility clinics and sperm banks. She always said it wasn't the right time, and because I loved her, I foolishly let her feed me that bullshit. But not anymore. I would no longer sacrifice my happiness for hers.

Traffic was a bit heavy, so I focused back on the road instead of getting lost in my thoughts. The last thing I needed was to rear-end someone and end up being late because of it. Whenever we had meetings, I liked to arrive before Tatiana. It didn't matter that we were best friends; I took my role as her personal assistant seriously. Tatiana had created an opportunity for me to earn a living, and because of her, I now owned properties, which further boosted my income. There aren't enough words in the dictionary to thank her for the kindness she extended to me and my sister. Besides being her assistant, Tatiana gave me a twenty percent stake in the spa—ten percent came from what she owned, and the other ten from Jonah's. Instead of dwelling on what Sav refused to give me, I threw myself into work. Now, here I was a few years later. Sav was in prison, and I was no closer to becoming a mother or wife.

Enough is enough.

CHAPTER FIVE

Jonah Cross

"WHAT THE HELL happened? I thought we were supposed to have a meeting."

I looked up as Yaya stormed into my condo. She was carrying her signature tote bag, with her hair pulled into a sleek, low bun and a worried expression on her beautiful face.

Damn, she's fine.

Tatiana was sitting at my dining table, holding a coffee mug filled with Coke and rum. She took a deep breath before glancing at her best friend, who was eager to know why the meeting had been canceled at the last minute and why she was instructed to come to my place.

"My father called and said someone tried to kill him. He thinks they might come after me and Nazira next. With Raphael gone, he believes everyone wants a piece of what we have," Tatiana explained, leaning back and looking stressed.

What started as an ordinary day turned chaotic as I rushed to Tatiana's condo, catching her right before she was about to shower, then hurriedly brought her and Nazira back to my place. I always protected them, but now I felt an even stronger duty since Karim was no longer here. I'd kill for them without hesitation.

Yaya flopped into a chair with her purse still on her shoulder, staring at Tatiana.

"Shit. Is he alright?"

"His security has taken him to a safe location until they can figure out who would want to hurt him."

I scoffed while pacing near the floor-to-ceiling windows overlooking FDR Drive and the Brooklyn Bridge.

"What's that supposed to mean?"

Yaya's voice drew my attention from the view to her sexy, pink, pouty lips.

"There's a long list of niggas who would want to get at his ass," I replied.

I could feel her doe-shaped eyes following my every move, but she quickly looked away when I turned to meet her gaze. Yalina liked to play games. She would try to act like she wasn't interested, but the way she sucked in her breath whenever I was near told me that she wanted me. One time, my body brushed against hers while I was grabbing a cup from the cabinet, and I swore I heard a moan escape her lips. It was no secret I wanted her just as much as she wanted me—well, maybe to her. I only allowed the games because I knew Yalina wasn't ready for what I was ready to give her, and one reason was because of Sav. She was the one thing standing in the way of Yalina and me having what we truly wanted—each other. Yalina, being the loyal type, I knew she wouldn't just leave her years-long relationship with Sav for an uncertain future with me. But I also knew—based on the phone conversations I overheard between them—that Yalina wasn't happy. Whenever I was around while she was on the phone with Sav, Yalina always sounded withdrawn and never excited.

"Jonah," Tatiana said, gently squeezing my forearm.

"Tati, I'm not going to front. Your pops has his hands in a lot of shit—some shit even Raphael didn't know about. So, there's no limit to who might want to hurt him," I said. Then, as I walked back over to the windows, I muttered, "Hell, I want to get at his ass, too," making sure to say it low enough so she wouldn't hear me.

I wasn't a big fan of Malcolm Rich, and honestly, I didn't trust him. He was always doing too much. Karim shared the same feeling when he was alive and wasn't crazy about the guy either. We only tolerated him because he was Tatiana's father. Malcolm may have clawed his way out of the trenches, but a nigga never forgets what he did to get to the top. He found a way to leech off every possible person higher up than him.

She groaned as I returned to her side. "Am I supposed to hide in the house for the rest of my life because of whatever he has going on?"

"No, but I'm getting security for you and Nazira. I'm not taking any chances."

Tatiana looked up at me. "Someone with us all the time, following behind us everywhere we go? You know how I feel about that. I argued Karim down about it."

"Um, that's what security is supposed to do, Tati." Yaya chuckled as she slipped her bag from her arm and placed it on the floor beside her feet. "Jonah is right. We don't know what your father is mixed up in, and with you basically being the head of the Sterling family, we can't take any chances when it comes to your safety."

I looked over at Yalina. "Well, I'm glad you agree—because you're moving into my crib in Greenwich so I can make sure you're safe, too."

She choked on her words. "Excuse you?"

I looked over at her while licking my lips. "Don't believe I fucking stuttered, Yalina. You live alone, and you're Tati's best friend. You don't think they would come at you, too? Shit, we don't even know who *they* are."

She folded her arms and poked that sexy-ass lip out. "You're not the boss of me, Jonah. I'm a grown woman who is capable of taking care of myself."

"I don't care how grown you are—I'm gonna make sure no harm comes to you. You can have all that 'independent woman' shit, but when you're in my presence, kill all that noise," I replied.

She looked away from me, breaking our intense staredown.

Tatiana looked at Yaya and then at me. "Am I interrupting something?"

"Nah," I responded, never taking my eyes off my baby.

She was trying hard not to look at me because she knew I was right. Sav was in prison and couldn't protect her. What was she going to do from behind bars? Hell, she hadn't done much of shit for Yalina besides stress her since she was sent away.

If she had listened and taken the damn lawyer I offered her, she wouldn't have gotten as much time as she did. Instead, she followed her paid lawyer's advice and is serving more. Sav's pride was as tall as Shaq, and that shit irritated me. Always puffing out her chest like she was the biggest thing walking the earth, but she was only put on because Karim had a soft spot for her. She was homeless and staying with friends until Karim offered to help change her life.

Tatiana sighed. "I guess I should call my father and ask him to send over some of his security for me and Nazira."

"Negative," I said, glancing at Yalina as I pulled out my phone to check the text message I received.

"What do you mean?" Tati questioned.

Yalina finally looked at me as I was replying to the text.

"Stop stressing, Yummy. I ain't got no bitches hitting this line. I'm respectful."

She snorted, crossed her arms, and rolled her eyes. "My name isn't Yummy. Where'd you even get that from?"

I smirked. "Let me test my theory first, then I'll tell you."

She shifted in her chair, clearly reacting to my words.

"Call me Yaya or Yalina. Pick one."

"Heard you, Yum," I replied while still smirking.

Tatiana looked at both before turning her gaze back to me. "I'm starting to feel like I'm interrupting something between you two."

"You're interrupting absolutely nothing, Tatiana. Jonah loves to get under my skin," she said, uncrossing her arms and looking away from me.

What I wanna do is get in your skin, I thought while checking my phone.

Tatiana rested her head on the table and sighed again. "What about Bloom?"

"She can stay with you. She already lives with you part-time," I replied, quickly sending another message before slipping my phone back into my pocket.

I gently rubbed Tatiana's back to comfort her. Just when it seemed like she was trying to move on after Karim's death, she was knocked back a few steps. Life was unfair to her, and I did everything I could to ease her stress.

When it came to the spa, I didn't hesitate to invest money and sit back. Even though Tatiana didn't finish college, the girl had brains, and I knew she could double my investment. Malcolm might have been a sleazebag, but I couldn't deny the man knew his shit. As his daughter, Tatiana watched and learned to be about her business, but Karim handled all the meetings because Tatiana hated that part. She preferred to play the back and see her vision come to life. I never had much to say about any decisions they made. As long as I was making back the money I invested, I didn't feel the need. But when my boy passed, I quickly stepped in to make sure Tatiana wouldn't have to take on his responsibilities. As much as suits made me uncomfortable and being around those stiff fucktards annoyed me, I sucked it up because my sister needed me.

"Why does Bloom get to stay with Tatiana, but you're forcing me to stay with you?"

I looked over at her. "I'm not *forcing* you to do shit, Yum. Just thought you would want your own space. You stayed in my guesthouse last year when your crib was being painted, and Nazira and Tatiana were sick."

"True," Tatiana chimed in.

"Girl, hush. You ditched us and only waved from outside the front door with soup because you didn't want to catch our germs. Just rude."

"I don't enjoy being sick. Nazira is forever bringing home some damn cold."

Yaya chuckled and crossed her legs. "Listen to us. Someone's trying to kill your father, and we're talking about catching colds. What's wrong with us?"

"Look, it's nothing you two need to worry about right now," I told them. "I just want to make sure you both are safe until I find out what's going on."

Yaya looked over at me. "Do you have your people looking into it already?"

I smirked. "You already know it, Yummy."

She rolled her eyes, shook off her trench coat, and pulled out her laptop from her bag.

"I'll reschedule everything and tell them it's a family emergency. Tati, do you want to go visit your father?"

Tatiana laughed. "After the last conversation we had? No, I'm fine knowing he's alive. No need to see him."

I left them in the kitchen and stepped out onto the terrace to make a call. If Malcolm thought I trusted his people to keep my girls safe, he thought wrong. I didn't trust his ass, and I sure as hell didn't trust the people he kept around him.

Sitting on the outdoor furniture, I held the phone to my ear. "Put the word out that I need his services."

"Bet," replied the person on the other end.

CHAPTER SIX

TEN YEARS AGO...

"Almost Doesn't Count" by Brandy

I SPUN AROUND as I felt the breeze caress my face, as we walked closer to the pier. Nazir had been on his phone for most of dinner, and that was normal for us. While he answered messages and calls, I just went along with the flow.

I've watched my mother deal with the same things. Except, with Nazir, it was slightly different. Each time he received a call or a text message, he would grab my hand and mouth his apology to me.

My father never apologized.

This trip was special because this was our first trip together. Nazir had surprised me with plane tickets and a hotel for a few days. Whenever he got an extra money, he almost always was ready to spend money on me.

He never cared that I came from money and could do all of those things for myself. Nazir was a man of pride, and he was going to always foot the bill. Our hotel was a few blocks from the beach.

We had eaten at a Mediterranean restaurant or dinner and decided to walk towards the beach. I could see in his face that he was stressed out with the way he was texting on his phone. Usually, I remained out of his business and allowed him to do what he felt was necessary. Tonight, I couldn't help but to ask what was going on, and who he was texting.

"Hey," I touched his hand, and he lowered his phone down, staring directly into my eyes. The fear and worry was etched into his brows.

"You had a good time tonight, Tata?"

I knew he was trying to prevent me from asking how he was doing. He didn't want to burden me with everything he had going on. Nazir was the kind of man that would keep everything bottled up and handle it on his own. He would never burden me with his problems, and I hated that.

A relationship was a give and pull thing. We should have been able to come to each other about our problems. I came to him whenever me and my father got into arguments. He was always there for me, and all I wanted was to be there for him.

"Dinner was delicious and anytime I get spend time with you is always a good time. I'm not talking about dinner, Nazir."

He looked out towards the ocean, as the sun was slowly setting in the background. Both the sunset and the ocean were competing, which made for a picturesque moment. As much as I wanted to pull my phone out and snap a few pictures, I was more concerned about my boyfriend.

"I got a lot going on right now, baby, the reason I wanted to take you away... wanted to spend some time with you."

I hugged him, while staring up at him. "I understand that, but you haven't been present… Naz, you have been everywhere but in this moment with me."

He bent down and kissed my lips. "And I apologize for that."

There was this look that I couldn't put my finger on. A sadness that consumed him when he stared down into my eyes. As if there was something he wanted to tell me, and he couldn't find the right words to convey the message.

"I want you to let me in. You tell me that I'm going to be your wife one day. Why keep things from me?"

His phone buzzed again, this time he ignored it.

"There's a lot of shit that I cannot talk to you about. This part of my life isn't up for debate, Tata. I want you to be my wife one day, but who knows if that will happen."

I ripped away from him and stared at him, tears threatening to fall because I couldn't picture a future without him.

I refused to have one without him.

Nazir was my comfort and the person who made me feel good about life. My life before him had been on autoplay and I was just living through it. When he entered my life, he showed me the other side of life.

A side that didn't consist of posh neighborhoods, jets, and expensive restaurants. Nazir showed me how the other side lived, and that everything wasn't always about money. He allowed me to see that I had lived in a bubble my entire life, and life had much more to give than living life like the Rich's.

He didn't treat me like Malcolm Rich's daughter like everyone else did. Nazir didn't care that I had a beautiful condominium or wore designer garb and knew which fork was used for a salad at dinner. All he cared about is if I was truly down for him like I had been for him.

"What the fuck do you mean who knows if that will happen?"

He tried to pull me back, but I stayed back because he had me messed up. Why were we wasting all this time if he didn't see us being together? He was allowed to be hesitant about things, but to actually hear it from his mouth irritated me.

"You already know how your father feels? Why you acting like this is shocking news to you. Tatiana, your father don't want you with a nigga like me."

He wasn't wrong. My father wanted me to marry a man from Greenpointe that was exactly like him. He wanted my future husband to come from a well to do family, so that our family remained connected to money.

All Malcolm Rich cared about was money. He would never approve of me and Nazir's relationship which is why I kept things private. I would have thought he would have been accepting being that Nazir came from humble beginnings like he did. My father loved to remind me that he had to claw his way up the ladder of success because he was raised poor.

He almost always forgot about that humble lifestyle speech whenever he was around his rich friends. None of that mattered, as he tried to fit in like he had always belonged within their circle.

"What did I tell you, Nazir?"

"Not trying to be the reason you fall out with your family, Tata."

"My family is already broken, Nazir. My mother and father's marriage is nonexistent, we don't take family vacations, and I barely visit home. My father would for sure cut me off, but I know my mother... she wouldn't cut me off and that's all I care about."

"Your mouth says that now."

"Why the fuck do you always try and tell me how I feel? I know exactly what I'm doing, Nazir, I'm not a stupid child."

We hardly got into arguments, however, whenever we did, he was always so calm and reserved while I was the lunatic. Like now, we were standing on this boardwalk while my hands were flailing in the air, and he was staring down at me. To someone walking past, I looked like a lunatic.

Resentment doesn't have a timeline. Right now, it seems cool to hate your father because he won't allow you to have your way. Years later when he's on his death bed, and you're staring at him in his last moments, Tata, you won't think of anything except the time you could have spent with him. You'll think of me, the reason that you stepped away from him. Baby, I don't want that for you."

I turned and walked away because the tears were burning my eyes. Nazir always had to make sense, even when I wanted to be irrational. As much as I didn't want to accept what he was saying, he wasn't completely wrong.

Me and my father didn't have the best relationship, but he was my father. There would come a time when I had to sit with my decisions and would I ate Nazir for them? Resent him because of decisions that I made?

With my arms folded I walked down the boardwalk, no longer concerned with the beach. I felt his hands wrap around me, and pull me towards him as I was mid-step.

"Let me talk to you real quick, Tata." His was gentle as he continued to pull me towards him, and I allowed him.

He slowly turned me around so I could look at him. The thing about Nazir was that he was so tall all I was staring at her was his chest. Lifting my chin up, he peered down into my eyes.

"Not everyone wants us together, baby. I need you to understand that. If someway we end up apart, I need you to know that I would rather die before ever leaving you… okay?"

"What are you not telling me?" I finally peered deeper into his eyes.

Finally seeing the look of worry, concern and regret. The regret was lingering in his eyes, like it hadn't happened yet, but he was already regretting it.

"I'm telling you the truth. I love you, Tata. I love you enough to tell you that."

A tear fell down my face, and he quickly wiped it away. "We don't need to worry about the future… let's worry about now."

"The future is important though. I want to be with you forever, Nazir… not just for now."

He kissed my lips a few times, holding the side of my face. "And I want the same thing. A nigga didn't spend all this money for us to be bickering."

I giggled because this vacation wasn't supposed to be about arguing. We needed to focus on us, and leave whatever we couldn't control away.

"I know and I'm sorry… can we start over."

"Don't ever apologize to me for you feelings, Tata… I love you, baby. Never question that, okay?"

"Okay."

CHAPTER SEVEN

Tatiana

IT HAD BEEN two days since I had gotten even an inch of sleep. Sleep didn't come easy after finding out someone wanted to kill my father. My relationship with my father wasn't the best, but I would never wish any harm on him. Malcolm Rich wasn't the nicest or easiest person to deal with; however, nobody ever wanted him dead—at least not to my knowledge. Plus, he was always surrounded by security because of our family's wealth. So, he wasn't an easy target.

I wasn't naive enough to believe Raphael and my father weren't involved in many illegal activities. Karim followed in his father's footsteps and kept me far removed from those things. He told me our marriage would only work if I didn't know how our family made our money, and I agreed. For years, I watched my father make business deals and travel across the country, but I never knew what he did. I always assumed he was just a businessman like my friends' fathers. All I knew was that I attended the best private schools, lived in the most expensive zip code, and always had money at my disposal. There was no limit to what I could ask for and receive.

It wasn't until I got older and started paying attention that I noticed the shady men who would come by our house to visit my father. Once, I witnessed one choke my father out while he sat behind his prized desk. The man got close to my father's face—their noses almost touching—and told him he wanted his money and wasn't going to keep playing around. That's when I started putting the pieces together and realized my family's reputation wasn't as clean as I thought. My father was involved in illegal things, and I had to keep my mouth shut about it. I was expected to always protect my father, and that's what I did. Always protecting him when he's never protected me a day in his life—pawning me off to another family for greed's sake. No matter how much time went by, I would never forgive my father for what he forced me to do.

"Mommy, why are you cleaning so much?"

Nazira skipped into the living room where I was vigorously wiping down the marble coffee table. She leaned against the couch while biting into an apple.

The housekeepers had just left the day before, so there was no need for me to clean the coffee table. But my nerves were frayed because of everything happening in our lives. My baby girl had no clue—and that's how I wanted to keep it. It was my job to protect her innocence. She didn't need to know about the life her father used to lead or what her grandfather still did, and I would do everything I could to make sure she never found out.

I looked over at her while straightening the couch pillows. "You look cute today," I said, avoiding her question. "That purple and blush look great together."

My baby spun around and smiled. "I needed a dramatic flair today—something that screamed drama. Mommy, when can I go back to school?"

She did a dramatic sulk and pretended to faint on the pillow I had just spent time fluffing.

It always amazed me how much personality my child had. I don't recall being as expressive and full of character when I was her age. She loved theater, and when she was younger, she would act out her favorite movies for Karim and me. He would clap so loudly for her, and she would wear this huge smile. Whenever she had a play, he was right there in the front row with flowers and his phone to record her. The box of phones on his side of the closet was filled with various videos and pictures of Nazira. Every time he got a new phone, he would never get rid of the old one. He would toss it into a box to keep the videos and pictures of our daughter. Karim was sentimental like that, caring about the small things.

I recall a time when he cut a work trip short to come home and take photos of Nazira opening her Christmas gifts. She was too young to even understand what a gift or Christmas was, but it was important to him. He wanted to be there to celebrate her first Christmas as a family. That's when I started falling deeper in love with him because he showed me that we were a priority—and canceling an important business deal to fly across the country just to see a baby drool over giftwrap proved that. *Oh, how I missed him.*

"Mom?"

I shook off my thoughts and looked at my daughter. "Hopefully, your godfather will let me know you can return soon. Where's Bloom?"

Nazira looked at me with a confused expression. "Mommy, Bloom hasn't been here all morning."

"Then who helped you get up this morning while I was in morning meetings?"

Nazira smiled. "Me. I told you I don't need a babysitter. I can take care of myself and get ready for the day."

Bloom had helped me with Nazira since she was a newborn, always there to support me. As a new mother, I was clueless, but

Bloom reminded me that it's okay not to know everything—which was new to me. I used to be someone who knew everything, and if I didn't know something, I would research it to find out. But no amount of baby books, articles, or classes could have fully prepared me for what I experienced during delivery and becoming a mother. Without my mother and Bloom's reassurance, I don't know what I would have done.

Yaya was there too, but she looked equally horrified at the newborn stage. Nazira spit up on her once, and she nearly passed out. It was funny because out of the two of them, Yaya always wanted to be a mother, while Bloom said she just wanted to be a rich aunt and wife, never a mom.

I checked my watch. "How about we watch a movie in the theater room?"

This morning, I spent most of my time on conference calls and replying to emails. With the resort in Las Vegas and a few in the Caribbean wanting to have Hush at their locations, I was preparing for traveling out of the country and trips to the West Coast. Bloom knew the situation; she also knew I was overwhelmed right now. There was so much happening, and I needed her to keep everything normal in Nazira's world. That's why I couldn't understand why she would leave without telling me. Curious, I sent her a text.

***Me:** Bloom, what the hell?*

***Her:** Had something to handle this morning. Zira told me that she could handle herself.*

I looked at my phone and sucked my teeth. Had I known my daughter was left unattended all morning, I would have canceled some meetings.

"Popcorn and pickles?" Nazira asked, jumping up happily.

I pretended to think with my finger on my chin. "How about jalapeños, or are you too scared of spice?"

She leaned her head on me and laughed. "Mom, I eat buffalo chicken now. I can handle a little bit of spice."

While Nazira went to pop us some popcorn, I quickly fixed the pillows she'd messed up and then went to the theater to grab our blankets and drinks. The house, over twenty thousand square feet, now felt too big with Karim gone. We had staff living in the guest houses in the back, yet the house often felt like it was swallowing me up whole—mainly because of its size and the unexpected grief that would hit me at every turn of the corner. Even simple tasks like showering or sweeping the sitting area could trigger waves of grief I couldn't shake, despite my breathing exercises. The bedroom no longer felt like a place of love. I slept on one corner of the bed, while my laptop, work bag, and other miscellaneous things took up space on the other side. It used to be my favorite room in the house. Now it reminded me of my loneliness and the possibility that I may never find love again.

I've loved and lost twice. Now, all I had were the good and bad memories that haunted me at night. Even though I knew I should start dating again, fear held me back. I was scared to open up and let someone see my hidden, deeper levels. I didn't want to risk having my heart shattered after letting my walls down.

Nazira and I cuddled on the couch as she pressed play on the remote to start her favorite movie, *Annie*. It wasn't the original *Annie* because Nazira couldn't relate to her. It was the black version of *Annie*. Besides relating to the actress because she was black, I wasn't sure what she meant by relate. The girl had never lived in an orphanage and had been born into wealth from the moment she took her first breath.

Watching a musical movie with Nazira meant knowing she would sing along at every opportunity. Yawning, I watched as she put on a show for only me. My eyelids became heavy as I watched her through slightly closed lids. The sleep I couldn't seem to find was finally catching up with me, and despite my efforts to stay awake, my eyes slowly closed completely and soft snores escaped my nose.

Nazira's singing and shouting had long stopped. Now I heard voices in the distance as I tried to get comfortable on the couch. When I couldn't find the right position, I gave up on trying.

"Zira, I'm sorry for falling asleep on you!" I shouted, not knowing where my child had gone.

Transformers was now playing on the screen, and Nazira was nowhere to be found. I sat up on the couch, slipped my feet into my house slippers, and wiped my eyes. I slept so hard I could feel the dried drool on the side of my cheek. It had been a while since I'd slept that soundly—only getting a few hours here and an hour there.

I rubbed my arms as I followed the voices, recognizing Jonah's voice immediately and knowing he was in the bar area of the theater room.

"Just need to keep my family safe when I'm not around. You see the size of this house—need to make sure whatever her father is into doesn't leak down to her."

I heard the clink of glass from the decanter, which meant he was making a drink.

"Keeping her safe is my priority," a voice replied.

That voice.

My heartbeat quickened as my pace slowed down. Holding onto the wall, I took several deep breaths while trying to calm myself. When I turned the corner, the air in my lungs escaped as I looked at him. He was holding his drink while still conversing with Jonah. Neither noticed me gripping the wall, silently panicking.

He wore a black short-sleeve shirt that squeezed his muscular arms, with tattoos wrapping around his biceps like ivy on an abandoned house. His side profile showed long lashes sweeping over his eyes like an umbrella over a picnic table. Those light brown eyes, when hit by the sun at a certain angle, looked greenish-brown. His beard, thick and lush with specks of gray, had grown out over the years, coarse black hair covering his face.

His forehead creased, revealing those wrinkles that would appear whenever he was engaged in a conversation. The expensive gold Patek watch that graced his wrist indicated that money was no longer an issue. The dance of the two colognes—one worn by Jonah and the other by Nazir. Even after years, I could still smell the cardamom and amber cologne as it tickled my nose. It was a scent I could never forget, one I spent many nights phantom-smelling because I swore he would sneak into my home and come save me.

My lip quivered as I watched them continue with their conversation. They were so engrossed that they still hadn't noticed me. So, I ducked back around the corner, and while leaning against the wall, I took another deep breath—this time sucking in the deepest breath my lungs would allow.

Despite the years that had gone by, this man still had that effect on me. His eyes hadn't even looked into mine, nor had his voice caressed my eardrums, yet my body reacted this way. But as much as he took my breath away, there was also a part of me that was furious.

Why is he in my home? And why is Jonah talking to him about protecting me and Nazira? Does he even know that Nazir and I know each other? I had many questions, but they could only be answered by asking.

Taking a deep breath, I shook off all the emotions and feelings I'd bottled up over the years and forced a neutral face—a face I'd developed since childhood when dealing with my father. There was no room for emotions when your father didn't give a damn about them.

Checking my hair in the hallway mirror, I used my nail to scrape the crust off the side of my face and then glanced at my clothes. Suddenly, I wished I had on something more flattering instead of the simple sweatsuit I wore since I was working from home that day. I took one last deep breath and spun around the corner.

"Jonah, why didn't you tell me you were here?"

My heart was pounding as I stood there with my hand on my hip.

He finished his drink and set the glass down. "Sent you an email this morning letting yo' ass know I was bringing security by today for you to meet."

Nazir turned his attention toward me, his eyes taking in all of me.

"Hi, Nazir. Nice to see you."

What else should I have said? It's good to see you're alive after abandoning me. Seeing him was bittersweet. It was sweet to know he was alive after years of wondering what had happened to him and if he was okay. But I felt bitter that he never reached out to check on me and had moved on with his life while I gave birth and raised our child.

Jonah looked between us. "You know each other?"

"We're old friends from my college days," I said. "Not important. Where's my daughter?"

"Bloom took her to get ice cream with the security team. I wanted you to meet Nazir, then I'll introduce you to the head of security who will stay with you at the house."

Nazir remained quiet, his thick lips protruding from his beard and mustache. His eyes were still as intense as the last time I had stared into them. Memories flooded my mind of him gazing into my eyes as he kissed me and told me he loved me.

Jonah's phone rang, and he looked at the number. "Let me take this real quick. Since you both know each other, catch the fuck up."

Neither of us laughed at Jonah's joke. Instead, Jonah followed me with his eyes as I sauntered behind the bar, grabbed the bottle of tequila, and poured myself a double shot.

"Tata—"

"No," I said, cutting him off.

The nerve of him to call me by a name I hadn't heard in a decade—a name only he had used. Hearing him say it transported me back to that college girl who wanted to spend forever with him.

"Baby—"

I held up my index finger to silence him as I threw back my drink.

Even as I stood behind the bar, discreetly squeezing the bottle while fighting to keep my composure, I wanted to run into his arms and feel them wrapped around me as he apologized. The old me would have tossed aside all the pain and hurt he caused, but the new me couldn't do that. Nazir had promised he'd never leave me. Yet, he did. He left me in the middle of the night, and I never heard from him again. It wasn't like I could go looking for him to find out why. And I didn't know his family, so I couldn't even reach out to them. Nazir knew so much about me, and I knew very little about him other than he handled his business and promised he wouldn't stay down for long. Now, standing in front of him, with his scent mesmerizing me, I saw that he kept one of his promises—never staying down for long.

I purposely checked my watch to signal he was on my time, and I didn't have much to give. It was something I learned from my father. He would do it whenever he wanted to send the message to someone that they weren't important or worth his time.

"Mr. Kane, you have no right to call me anything but Mrs. Sterling. This is strictly business, and your job here is to protect my family—nothing more. We're two strangers from our past, and that's how we'll remain. Thank you for taking us on as clients," I said, reaching across the bar to shake his hand, which he accepted.

I slid my hand into his large hand, and I gave the firmest handshake I could. My hand trembled slightly because his touch still incited the same emotions inside me.

"Mom! I bought you back some butter pecan ice cream," I heard my daughter singing as she came running down the stairs, and my heart jumped in my chest.

Here I was trying to stay professional with a man I shared a child with—a man who didn't know he had a child who was literally his namesake.

Nazira zoomed around the corner and crashed right into my arm, holding a bag of ice cream.

"Thank you, baby. You know how much I love butter pecan."

She looked up at me with a smile she shared with her father—the man who was sitting across from us. "Bloom wanted to make it up to you."

I laughed because Bloom knew I was upset with her. She knew she shouldn't have left without at least telling me that she was leaving, so she was going to do whatever she could to get back in my good graces.

"Oh, really?"

Nazira laughed. "Just forgive her, Mom. She's really sorry."

I kissed her forehead a few times and brushed her curls out of her face.

"Oh shit."

The voice snapped me back, reminding me that Nazir was there and watching us.

Nazira turned and smiled at him. She stayed at my side, but she was now focused on Nazir.

"Hi, I'm Zira. Who are you?" she asked.

"Hi, Ms. Zira. I'm part of the security team that's going to keep you safe. My name is—"

"Baby," I quickly interrupted Nazir, handing her the bag, "why don't you run upstairs and put this in the freezer before it melts?"

"Okay, Mommy," she said before skipping off.

I took a slight breather, then slowly turned my attention back to Nazir, who was staring a hole through me.

"Tata… my mom has the same birthmark."

"It's Mrs. Sterling. And a lot of people have the birthmark Zira has," I quickly defended, then poured another shot and threw it back, unbothered by the burning in my throat.

Nazira had a distinctive birthmark on the side of her face. I never knew where it came from; I just saw it as part of my beautiful baby's uniqueness. It never crossed my mind that it could be hereditary. Nazira loved her birthmark and had never struggled with accepting it.

"Who's her father, Tatiana?" he asked.

I quickly stepped from behind the bar. "I'm not getting into—"

"Tati, I've got to run real quick," Jonah said, coming from the back. "Some shit is always happening."

I exhaled, relieved that the interruption had saved me from having to answer Nazir.

"Is everything alright?"

Jonah kissed the side of my head. "Yeah. Some shit is always happening, and I need to make sure shit's straight."

"Be careful, Jonah," I reminded him, as I always did.

"You already know."

"Take your company with you."

Jonah looked between me and Nazir. "I take it the past between you two wasn't the best."

Ignoring him, I headed upstairs to plow my way through the ice cream Nazira had brought home for me. When I hit the top step, I saw Bloom was at the kitchen counter on her phone. Noticing me, she quickly ended her call and smiled.

"Tati, I know you're mad at me, but—"

I raised my hand. "Water under the bridge. Just tell me next time."

She let out a deep sigh. "Thank God you're not… Wait a minute. This is almost too easy. Who died?"

Jonah came upstairs with Nazir behind him.

"Who's that?" Bloom asked as I scooted past her to reach the fridge.

Bloom batted her eyelashes but then widened her eyes after getting a better look. Both Bloom and Yaya knew what a younger Nazir looked like from the pictures I showed them. Not much about his appearance had changed, except that he became finer with age and had a few gray hairs.

She cleared her throat and grabbed her tote that was on the counter.

"Um, hey Jonah," she quickly greeted, then made herself scarce, but not before giving me a confused look once she was behind Nazir.

A Spanish man with a bald head and tattoos covering his muscular arms entered the kitchen. He had a scowl that could send even the meanest man cowering. He nodded to Nazir, then approached the counter and extended one of his tattooed hands.

"Hi, I'm Emilio. I'll be head of security for you and your daughter. Jonah has given me the rundown, and I can assure you that you and your seed are safe with me."

My seed? Using that lingo, I could tell this was a man who grew up in the hood, and if I had to put any bets on my safety, it would be with him. The gun tucked in the back of his waistband told me everything I needed to know.

Just then, Bloom peeked her head back into the kitchen. "I can take Zira to school in the morning if she's going back."

Emilio looked at Bloom, and I could've sworn I saw his cheeks turn red from blushing. His eyes were locked on her, then he glanced over at Nazir, who nodded in response. They both understood what it meant because Emilio left the kitchen and headed down the hall without saying another word.

"She can return to school," Jonah replied before I could even gather my thoughts.

When it came to Nazira, Jonah didn't play. I prayed for the day she decided to start dating and for whoever the young man would be, because I knew her godfather would give him hell.

Bloom nodded. "Sounds good. I'll take her."

"Security will accompany you two," he said, never looking up from his phone. "I'm heading out. I'll walk you out, Nazir."

Nazir walked past me, his scent wafting through the air and overwhelming my senses.

"It was nice seeing you, Mrs. *Sterling*."

I could tell from his tone that he didn't take my new last name seriously. When we were together, I was Ms. Rich, and had he never abandoned me, I would have been Mrs. Kane. Who knows where our lives would've gone together? One thing was certain: we would have been parents.

Jonah looked at both me and Nazir and laughed.

"Was shit really that fucked up to be on a last name basis?"

When neither of us responded, he shrugged his shoulders and left the kitchen with Nazir following behind him. As soon as they were gone, I took a deep breath and leaned on the counter. Bloom spun around the corner and nearly hopped onto the kitchen island to hear what I had to say. We waited a moment, listening to the chime of the front door, before exchanging a "Girl, what the hell" look.

"We cannot wait for Yaya to dig into whatever just happened."

She was leaning halfway across the island, her eyes trained on me. She followed every move I made.

The drink I had downstairs didn't have any effect, so I grabbed a bottle of wine from the wine fridge and popped it open. Taking two glasses, I poured nearly the entire bottle into my cup and handed Bloom what was left.

"Years have passed, and I moved on, never thinking I would see him again. I've spent years trying to forget him, and now… now he appears."

I was speaking to both Bloom and myself. These were the thoughts that filled my head when I saw him sitting downstairs. Bloom sipped her wine, giving me the chance to ramble a bunch of words that eventually stopped making sense. When I was done, she slid my full glass of wine toward me.

"Take a sip and breathe for crying out loud."

I grabbed the glass, leaned on the counter, and slowly sipped the merlot that wasn't doing anything to calm my racing heart.

"I never expected to see him again. I had gotten used to the idea of never seeing him ever again. I even started thanking God that I wouldn't have to have that conversation with him."

"Who says you have to?

I looked at Bloom like she was drinking something stronger than aged merlot.

"I can't have this man around here, knowing we share a daughter, and not tell him. He already asked about her birthmark."

"What about her birthmark?"

"Apparently, his mother has the same birthmark."

Bloom leaned back in the chair as she sipped her wine. "So, his mother has the same birthmark. Why didn't you mention that before?" she questioned.

I remained leaning on the counter while staring at her. At times, I cut her slack because she was often out of the loop. While Yaya and I were known for popping a bottle of wine and cuddling up on the couch for deep conversations that always ended with us crying in each other's arms, Bloom was the complete opposite. She wasn't emotional like us, and whenever we had a girls' night, she was almost always somewhere doing something else. When she did join us, her advice was always fuck everything and everybody. Sometimes her advice was solid, but not always—and especially when it came to her understanding how I felt about losing Karim. She assumed, because he had been gone for some time, that I would move on with my life and not grieve so much.

As much as I looked like I was carrying everything well—and for the most part I was—there were times when I wasn't. That's when I needed someone to tell me it was all right. My mother wasn't that person because she was off living her own life, and I would never hold that against her. For years, she sacrificed her happiness for her family—always showing up and being the rock because my father never cared to. Now it was her turn to be free and in love with someone who actually showed her love in return. I wanted nothing but the best for my mother, and that meant not giving up more of her life to move in with me because my husband died—although she tried.

"Girl, you just spaced." Bloom waved her hands in my face, and I looked over at her.

"Sorry. What were we talking about?"

She set down her wine glass. "Birthmark and your ex-boyfriend from college being in your home."

I sighed. "I never met Nazir's family. He was always closed off about that side of his life, and I respected that. I never brought him around mine either."

"So, you both treated each other like side people? Tati, the man could've been married for all you knew."

"He wasn't married. Nazir wouldn't lie and betray me like that… I don't think." I lifted my glass and took a slow sip.

The Tatiana I was in college wanted to believe he would never do something like that to me. That whatever made him leave, he did it because he had to—not just to hurt me.

"Girl, he could've had a wife, a child on the way, and been the mayor of Bloomville."

"Bloomville?"

"Not important," she replied with a wave of her hand. "My point is, he's not the same man you fell for when you were in college. So much life has happened since then. Neither of you are the same people."

"He saw her, Bloom. He's going to put the pieces together."

"And you're gonna have to be honest with him." She paused for a moment. "Actually, he abandoned you with a child, so you don't owe the nigga nothing."

I snorted. "He had no clue I was pregnant when he left."

She folded her arms across her chest as if she wasn't convinced. "Yeah, well, he damn sure ain't checked in on you since he left you butt naked and full of cum."

"Bloom!" I threw the wine cork at her, laughing.

She ducked and started laughing, too.

"He works for the security firm," I said once I caught my breath. "So luckily, I don't have to deal with him. Jonah will more than likely handle everything security-related."

"Jonah wants to handle everything, hmm?"

I chuckled. "Well, your sister has set clear boundaries and doesn't want anything to do with him."

"Yalina has always been stupid when it comes to what's good for her. What does she think is gonna happen when Sav comes home? They're gonna braid each other's pussy hair and live happily ever after?"

I choked on my wine, bending over the counter as I coughed. "Bloom! Why would you say that?"

Bloom tucked her feet under her and shrugged. "Sav isn't in love with Yalina. She likes the control and bragging rights. Do you know how many niggas want Yalina? Sav knows that. That's why she keeps her claws in her."

It was rare for me to agree with Bloom, but she wasn't wrong. Sav was in love with the control and status she got from being with Yaya. Yaya was loyal, and if she gave you her word, you could take it to the bank. That's just who she was—and Sav knew it. But there were many nights when she cried to me about being tired and not being in love with Sav. Still, she stayed.

Bloom's phone rang, and she glanced at it before hopping down from the stool. "We're good here?"

I saw my own phone ringing and recognized the family's lawyer's number. I ignored the call. I had enough going on and didn't have the mental capacity to deal with anything else at the moment.

"Yeah," I replied, continuing to slowly sip my wine as my mind drifted to the ghost from my past, someone I never expected to see again.

CHAPTER EIGHT

Nazir Kane

I WRAPPED MY lips around the tightly rolled spliff and took a long pull before blowing the smoke out the window and leaning my head back on the headrest in my Rolls-Royce, thinking about when Tatiana made her presence known. Her hair was all undone, sleep still in her eyes—and the pain. Before she could hide it, I saw the pain in her eyes as she stared into mine. I put that pain there, and it's something I would never forgive myself for.

Before she could fully step behind the bar counter, I took in her curvaceous shape. Tatiana had always been on the thicker side, and it only got better with the older she became. Her button nose was slightly red, and her freckles were visible because she wasn't wearing any makeup. Then there were her eyes,—her beautiful brown mahogany eyes. Tatiana's eyes were like windows to her soul. I could always tell her mood from the way she looked at me. When she was happy, it almost seemed like her eyes were closed because her smile was that wide. When she was sad, they looked dark and gloomy. The redness showed whenever she was emotional.

I spent a lot of time studying the woman I wanted to marry back then. Tatiana was a few years younger than me and had her whole life ahead of her. I knew how much she wanted to get married and have children. I wanted those things with her, too—but when I was in a better place. She deserved to be taken care of, and I couldn't do that for her—at least not then. So, that night, I decided not to hold her back any longer from having the things her heart desired. I kissed her lips, squeezed her tightly, then slipped out of bed and left in the middle of the night.

It still pains me that I hurt her the way I did. I stood by that door for twenty minutes, debating whether to leave or rejoin her in bed. As much as I wanted to run away with her and start a new life together, I knew it wouldn't be fair to her. Taking her from a life she was accustomed to, only for her to struggle being with me, would have never sat right in my spirit.

Tatiana thought she was keeping her life separate from her father, but once she mentioned his name, I knew who that nigga Malcolm was. Everybody in the hood knew him as the one who made it out. Niggas without any sense idolized him because he rose to a status. To them, he was the goat and someone they all wanted to be. They never knew the heads he stomped on to reach that level, but some of their own families knew the pain Malcolm Rich caused to get there. Nine times out of ten, they had an uncle hanging out in front of the corner store who should have been where Malcolm was, but they were greased and burned by him. I never respected him or looked at him as being a role model because I saw him for who he was at a young age.

My pops was greased and sent to prison because of Malcolm Rich's bitch ass. My mother was robbed of the life she once had, leaving her forced to work three jobs to make sure her two children had whatever they needed. While other kids were focused on sports or dreaming of going to college so they could be successful and make their parents proud, I was in the streets—learning the game from my pops during prison visits or through coded phone calls.

When the rumors started swirling about the dirt Malcolm had his hands in, my father was set up and murdered behind the wall. What was "cleaning up dead ends" for Malcolm was pure hell for my family. My old man never coming home was a harsh reality I had to accept early on in life, but seeing the pain on my mother's face replayed in my mind often.

When I first met Tatiana, I had no idea her father was Malcolm Rich or that she was related to him. Her last name didn't set off any alarms because it was a common name. But after finding out, it didn't change how I felt about her. I think it was because she didn't act like her father. She never walked around like the world owed her something. She was humble, quiet, reserved, and caring. Tatiana would give you whatever she had if she knew you needed the shit. That's why I fell for her before I even knew who she was. And that's why I stayed even after I found out where she came from and who her father was. Everything inside me told me to leave her alone. Her father was someone I wanted dead; how could I love his daughter the way I do?

Even as I sat in my car smoking, my heart was beating crazy in my chest because she was near. She was back in my orbit again, and my heart only reacted this way with her. She was my earth, moon, and stars.

The passenger door opened, and Natalie got in.

"You've been sitting out here for the past hour, Nazir. What's wrong?" she asked, turning toward me.

Natalie was another one of those women who I couldn't give the love she needed. Although I desperately wanted to, I didn't want to waste her time. So, I was honest with her, and she ended up becoming my best friend—the one I could turn to when the world felt like it was crashing in on me. She was the woman who held my secrets and helped me work through my depression. Most of those years after leaving Tatiana were spent in darkness, trying to talk myself through things.

Seeing the concern in her eyes, I knew I needed to ease her worries and allow her to breathe.

"I'm not on the edge, Nat."

She let out a deep sigh, leaned her head against the window, and reached over to touch my hand.

"You can't show up in the middle of the night, sit out here for hours, and expect me not to worry."

As the head of my family, the man who made things happen and made sure everyone was okay, who could I turn to? Who rubbed my back when I needed to release and express my emotions? I hated to go to my mother because she had to be strong for so many years, and I didn't want that for her anymore. All the pain she endured when my father was sentenced and then getting the call from prison that he had been murdered was just too much for her to bear. With my sister being old enough to understand what had happened, she experienced those same emotions. They both deserved to live a life free of emotional pain, and I worked hard to make sure they did.

Shit, I hated that Natalie was even the one I sometimes dumped my emotional baggage on, but she was my person—the one who put her own wants and needs aside to be there for me. There wasn't enough money in the world to pay her for what she had been to me.

"I wanted to come in and see her, but I didn't want to wake her up. I know the rules and the schedule," I said with a smirk, taking one last pull before putting out my blunt and flicking it out the window.

She squeezed my hand. "The rules don't apply when it comes to you needing to see her. Trust me, I know that feeling, and I'm lucky to have her just down the hall from me."

Nazani was four years old and my heart in this ruthless world. She was the good I needed when I was out here being anything but. If I wasn't with my baby girl, I was thinking about her. When Natalie asked if I would go half on a baby with her, I didn't have to think twice. If I couldn't give her my heart, the least I could do was give her one to carry.

Parenting with Natalie was like a warm breeze on a beach—easy. The breeze understood its role and how to coexist peacefully with the beach because both knew their parts. We had agreed on this and wanted a child, so there were never any issues.

Natalie had a nigga she was messing with, but she refused to allow him to meet me or our daughter. If she wanted to continue dating Casper in private, I didn't have a problem with it. Her love life wasn't my business. As long as whoever he was treated both Natalie and my daughter right, he would never have to worry about any smoke from me.

Natalie had been around when I was just trying to get money and keep it. She never looked at me any differently, so when I started getting real money, I made sure she never had to ask for shit—that she and my daughter lived an easy life.

She wasn't the type to sit around and let someone take care of her, though. Like me, she was used to getting it out the mud. It was Natalie who told me the only way this would work was if she had her own income, which she earned being a mommy influencer and blogger. I damn near had to twist her arm to get her to agree to buy the house in Greenwich Pointe. For me, it was less about providing for Natalie and more about providing for our daughter. I grew up in Brooklyn, in the hood—never experienced gated communities and private schools. My daughter would have all of that. I wanted her far removed from the city. The life I lived in the streets was ruthless, and I would never put my daughter in harm's way. So, whenever I wanted to spend time with my baby girl, I always came to Greenwich.

My mother and sister lived in Belgrave Hills, which was only a fifteen-minute drive between cities, and keeping them safe was my top priority. I refused to ever have to bury them because of my actions. It was the one promise I made to myself when I decided to step fully into this life. I've always dabbled—made enough money to be comfortable and help my mother quit one of her three jobs—but this life was never supposed to define me. I never wanted to end up like my father.

When he was murdered, my mother fell into a deep depression, and I knew I had to step up. Still, I was never all the way in. Just long enough to make some bread, then I'd pull back out.

With Tatiana, I always knew she came from money, but when the pieces connected, it made sense—and it made me want to do more. The money I made was split between her and my family. My family came first, and agreeing to leave with Tatiana would've meant leaving them behind—and dragging her into a life she knew nothing about. That would have been unfair to her, so I left so she wouldn't have to make the decision of picking me over her family.

The sound of the car door opening pulled me from my thoughts.

"Come inside. You look tired. She'll be up in a few hours, and I know she will be excited to spend every second with you."

"You got shit planned in the morning?"

"I do. I have a few meetings with this local coffee shop in town. The owner is a single mother, and I want to highlight her on the blog. A single *Black* mother," she emphasized while lifting her brows.

I chuckled and killed the engine before climbing out of the car.

"Everything is Black in this town—the only wealthy area I actually feel safe and seen."

"We're the majority, and I love it here. Although I hate to admit that last part."

We both paused, and she busted into a fit of giggles.

"Go ahead and tell me. Tell me I'm right, Natalie."

"I refuse."

"Nah, 'cause you fought me tooth and nail about moving here."

She continued to laugh. "Your mom and sister only being fifteen minutes down the road helps a lot, too. Zareena actually called me the other day. She wanted to take Zani to get some ice cream."

"Oh yeah? She never answers that damn phone when I call," I said, raising my eyebrow as I followed behind Natalie.

My tall frame swallowed her 5'3" figure. Natalie, petite and curvy, often got annoyed about always being the short person. It was a known rule never to mention her height. It was the reason she always wore heels—if she wasn't, she would complain about feeling naked without them.

As soon as I crossed the threshold, the scent of eucalyptus and jasmine consumed me, making me relax my jaw and shoulders. Natalie was into all that wellness bullshit, and even though I called it bullshit, the shit worked.

"Breathe in, and I'll make us some tea, because clearly you got something on your mind," she said before turning and walking off toward the kitchen, leaving me in the foyer.

I kicked off my sneakers and headed in the opposite direction to the sunken living room with a huge sectional that always drew me in. I don't know how many nights I ended up in Natalie's driveway, and she always welcomed me in. The couch was my spot, and it's where my daughter would find me when she woke up.

After pulling my shirt over my head, I flopped onto the couch with my feet up on the chaise. I closed my eyes, and images of that little girl flooded my mind.

Zira.

She looked so much like Tatiana, but she also resembled Nazani with her curly hair and the dimple on her cheek. She also had the exact birthmark that my mother had, and I hadn't met many people with the same.

I didn't miss the look on Tatiana's face when her daughter rounded that corner and ran into her arms. She looked like she wanted to disappear into thin air and refused to look me in the eyes. I had a nagging feeling that little girl was my daughter. Not to mention, she reminded me of Zareena when she was younger.

"Alright, no sugar and just a dash of honey."

Natalie placed the tea down on a coaster while getting cozy on the other end of the couch. Then she tossed her throw across her legs and took a sip of tea from her mug.

"Why are you awake at this hour?" I asked.

"I was doing some last-minute work and couldn't sleep much. My homie and I have been going at it lately."

I snorted. "Does homie have a name, Nat?"

She giggled. "You don't need to know that until I'm sure. I feel like I'm sure, but then there are things that keep me on the fence. Anyway, I'm not the one who showed up in your driveway. What's going on?"

"I saw her."

Natalie casually blew on her tea. "Who? Please don't tell me it's that chick you couldn't get rid of."

"Tatiana."

Her eyes widened. "*Thee* Tatiana Rich?"

The moment I couldn't give Natalie what she needed in terms of love and a relationship, she wanted to know the woman behind my reason. I told her daily she should have been a therapist with the way I would lay on her couch and share everything I was feeling. I was able to cry and be vulnerable when I was in her space. That was something I couldn't do or be out in the world. My clients paid me big money to protect their families and knew my reputation, which is why they had no problem sending over seven figures to ensure their family's safety. What would I look like crying on the job or discussing my personal shit?

When I first started, it was just me. I was the nigga who went from state to state—even out of the country—with whatever family had the best price. Over the years, I built a team of solid men who could ensure the safety of my clients.

I knew Jonah from around the hood. We didn't know each other personally, but we knew about each other. We would acknowledge each other and keep it at that. When he sent word through the grapevine that he needed security for his family, I reached out to him to see what he was talking about.

Jonah Cross's money was long, but little was known about his movements or whether he had a family. His vague explanation about needing to protect his goddaughter and her mother caught me off guard. He invited me to meet with her, and that's when I saw the love of my life. The woman I should have married had been asleep under the same roof as me for nearly an hour, and I hadn't known. Nor did I know I was sharing a drink with her best friend.

"Yeah."

"How did the two of you end up crossing paths?" Natalie was now fully invested.

"It was only a matter of time. Her father is in the life, and I heard she married into it, too. That's all I knew because I purposely didn't go looking for her."

She sighed. "Well, what did you say to her, Nazir?"

I watched as she tucked her legs underneath her and watched me closely.

"I didn't get to say much because she made it very clear that things would stay strictly business between us. But I could see she was hurt. The shit was easier to deal with when I didn't have to look into her eyes."

"Well, you have to face the consequences of your actions that you made years ago. We all have to answer for the decisions we make."

"She was pregnant with my baby."

Natalie had just started to sip her tea when I blurted out those words, causing her to spit it all over the coffee table, with some hitting my arm. I was so numb that the liquid hitting my arm didn't bother me.

"What do you mean?"

"She has a daughter, and I think she's mine. Nat, she has the same dimple as Nazani and the same birthmark as my mother. She looks like a younger Zareena."

"Whoa."

"Yeah."

"Did you ask her?"

"I tried, but she brushed me off before I could get the words out. Then she quickly left the room."

Natalie sighed again. "The good thing is that you have someone as her security, so you can keep your distance and approach this gradually. If that little girl is your daughter, it means Nazani has an older sister, and we want to approach this—"

"I can't approach this gradually. If she's my daughter, I've wasted too much time already. Feel me?"

"Yeah, I get tha—"

"Dada,"

I looked over the couch at my daughter who was standing in the doorway holding her favorite blanket and teddy bear.

"Hey, baby, you wanna sleep with Daddy?"

Nazani quickly rushed into the living room and around the couch. She climbed up and jumped onto me, resting her head on my chest. I placed her blanket over her and kissed her forehead.

"Missed you, mamas."

"Missed you too, Dada," she yawned sleepily, rubbing her eyes as I gave her a gentle squeeze.

Natalie smiled. "We'll continue this conversation another time. Get some sleep, you two."

She grabbed her cup and quickly cleaned up her mess. Before leaving the living room, she nuzzled Nazani's curls and kissed her head. I did the same, watching her softly snoring as I rubbed her back.

I never understood my role in this life until I became a father. Nazani Kane made me realize what I was meant to do: to love and protect her with my life. I loved being a dad and didn't know what the fuck I was doing before I became one. If Tatiana's daughter was indeed mine—which I strongly suspected she was—that meant I missed out on years with her. Tatiana went through this alone, and for that, I doubted she would ever forgive me.

Fuck.

CHAPTER NINE

Tatiana

THE SUN CREEPING through my windows should have been a sign that I needed to start my day, except I had beaten the sun rising for the third morning in a row. I found myself waking up in the middle of the night, tossing and turning until I finally admitted to myself that sleep would be the last thing I would get.

My sleep schedule hadn't been the best since Karim passed, but after seeing Nazir the other day, it had gone from terrible to shit. All the memories I forced out of my mind had come rushing back in. His scent hadn't left my nostrils, and he hadn't been inside my house in over seventy-two hours, but who's counting?

Before I wasted hours recounting every memory I shared with Nazir, I climbed out of bed and began my morning routine. Whenever I was in Greenwich Pointe, I alternated between working out in my home gym and going to town to exercise with Yaya and our personal trainer.

Yaya had been in her own world, which wasn't anything new. Apart from me sending her brief text messages about how I was feeling, we hadn't discussed it. Not because she didn't rush over to check on me, but because I needed to put it out of my mind.

I looked into Bloom's room and saw her tossed across the bed, still asleep. Before heading downstairs, I checked Nazira's room and saw she was still asleep, as well. She had about an hour before it was time for her to wake up for school.

The security team Jonah had hired was already on duty, so it wasn't unusual for me to run into one of them on my way down the steps. It was a bit of an adjustment, considering I was used to being the only one awake at this hour, sitting in silence alone.

Emilio, the head of security for our family, was usually found in the downstairs office. It used to be Karim's office, but I cleaned it out a year after his death. Every time I tried to do it before then, I would break down in tears while sitting behind the desk. The memories and passing by it every day were too painful for both me and Zira. His office had become a mausoleum of memories. It housed all his pictures, degrees, and anything else that meant something to him. Whenever I needed to feel close, I would creep down there, sit in his chair, and look through old family pictures. I'd have a good cry and then close the doors to continue with life.

"Good morning, Mrs. Sterling. The car is ready for you, and a guard is already waiting," he said, standing with tired eyes but refusing to rest.

The guest bedroom on this level was free for them to use. Karim's office was now filled with monitors and advanced security systems that seemed too complex for me to understand.

"It's Tatiana, Emilio. You're going to be around my family often, so we can skip the formalities."

He smiled. "Thank you for the food last night. We appreciate it."

Usually, when I cooked, I made small portions for myself, Bloom, and Nazira. Bloom usually went out to dinner, so it typically ended up being just the two of us. Last night, I cooked enough to feed Emilio and the two guards who were also protecting the house.

I had to insist they sit down and share a meal with us. They eventually agreed, but not without keeping an eye on their phones connected to the security system. They unplugged as much as needed, and it was a pleasant dinner. Afterward, Nazira acted out a part in her upcoming play, which earned her a standing ovation she couldn't stop raving about while going down for bed.

"Don't expect home-cooked meals every night, because I'm the queen of ordering takeout. But thank you for making my baby smile. She couldn't stop talking about her standing ovation."

He chuckled. "You're very welcome. Shall we?"

I quickly went to fill my favorite water bottle and grabbed my gym bag as Emilio held the door open for me. The second guard at the back door of the car opened it for me.

"Thanks, Anthony."

"You good, Tatiana. Enjoy your workout," he said, closing the door as I finally settled into the butter-soft leather.

I would never admit it to Jonah, but it felt nice having security around. With it being just me and Nazira most of the time, the house didn't feel as big with them there. As the car drove down our long driveway and passed through the neighborhood gates, I closed my eyes, hoping for a quick ten-minute nap.

"Good morning, Tata."

My eyes sprang open, and I stared at the driver.

Nazir was dressed casually in a white T-shirt and a durag. It felt like my body finally registered something because his signature scent filled the car as soon as our eyes locked through the rearview mirror.

"You're not my driver. Where's my driver?" I asked.

"Until everything is cleared with your father, Jonah doesn't want anyone your father hired to work for you."

I took a deep breath. "And let me guess… you do this for all your clients, huh?"

He easily maneuvered the Maybach through the posh streets of Greenwich. Nazir didn't belong in Greenwich Pointe. I had spent so much time keeping our relationship hidden from Greenwich. I've always felt like Nazir was too genuine for this town.

I should have noticed him before he spoke, since his seat was nearly in the back with me to accommodate his height.

"I haven't stopped thinking about you since the other day."

"And what do you want me to do with that information? Want me to jump into your lap, excited that you thought about me after all these years?"

What I wanted was to jump out of the car as he kept cruising, intentionally doing the speed limit to give us more time for this awkward conversation I didn't want to have. I used to imagine how the conversation would go if I ever saw him again. Would I slap the hell out of him or rush into his arms because I had missed him so much?

My heart ached for this man as if it were a death. I mourned him and drove myself crazy trying to figure out where he had gone and why. The man I knew wouldn't have abandoned me the way he did. A small part of me blamed myself for him leaving. Maybe if I hadn't pushed, he wouldn't have disappeared on me.

"You never left my mind, Tata."

"Stop calling me that," I replied firmly.

He wasn't allowed to call me that. It was a name rooted in love, and now I wasn't sure if what we had was even real. Someone who loved me as Nazir claimed he did wouldn't have done what he did without an explanation.

Closure.

"Tata, I know what I did was fucked up, and I don't think I could ever make it right. But I want the chance to try."

My eyes welled up, and my voice cracked as I stared at the side of his face.

"You can never make this right, Nazir. Why do you think you can just pop back into my life and try to make everything right? Huh? What gives you the right to believe you can do that?"

My hands were balled up, and my face burned with anger. *How does he think he can fix this? There's nothing he can do to make this right.*

"I don't have the right, baby. But us crossing paths again wasn't a coincidence. It was meant to happen. It was meant to confirm everything I've spent years thinking about. A nigga doesn't deserve the chance I'm asking for, Tata. I know and understand that. But—"

"Stop," I whimpered.

My heart was pounding so loudly I could hear it in my ears, and my vision was blurred from the tears that were begging to fall down my cheeks. I didn't want to hear what he had to say because it wouldn't make the situation better. Nothing could erase the fact that I had been forced to raise my daughter in a lie. Karim was who Nazira knew as her father. How was I supposed to look into her eyes and tell her that this stranger was her real father?

"I fucked up, and I have my reasons for why I left. All I ask is for you to give me a chance to explain."

As we neared the gym, I silently thanked God. All my hidden emotions were surfacing, and I felt an overwhelming urge to get out of the car and away from him. Nazir didn't deserve to see me cry. I was angry at myself for even being on the verge of tears. That was something I promised myself I'd never do over him again. I had spent so many years crying for a man who had left me. When I stared into my daughter's face on the happiest day of my life, I felt sorrow because he wasn't there to witness her being born. In my head, he had not only abandoned me; he had abandoned both of us.

As soon as he pulled up at the gym, I quickly gathered my things and reached for the handle. I wanted to get the hell away from him, and I needed to do it immediately. I was two minutes from breaking down and revealing all the bottled-up anger, resentment, and love I still harbored for him.

I was supposed to hate this man, but as I stared into his chocolate eyes, that emotion eluded me. I couldn't hate him, and I hated myself for not being able to do what should have been simple. I should've been able to hate him easily. Months ago, it was unthinkable that I'd be on the verge of tears and wanting to jump out of a moving vehicle because of him. I had been doing a better job of being in control of my emotions, yet here I was, spiraling in front of the man who had sent me down this emotional path.

Yaya stood outside the gym, looking confused as she stared into the car window, wondering why I hadn't gotten out yet. The car's tint was too dark for her to see inside.

"Jonah hired you to protect me and my daughter. I'd appreciate it if you did that and left the other bullshit out of the equation. Past mistakes don't matter; what matters is the present, and we have to live with our decisions, no matter how hurtful they are."

I reached for the door handle, got out, and slammed the door without looking back. All it took was for Yaya to take one look at me, and she instantly knew something was wrong.

"What happened, Tati?"

I blew past her and into the gym, heading straight to the bathroom in the back. My nerves were frazzled. I didn't know what to do. *Why did he get into that car this morning thinking this was a good idea? That we would have a conversation, and he would be able to smooth everything over. It was stupid of him to even think I would want to spend a second with him.*

I locked the door and leaned on the granite bathroom counter, taking a few deep breaths. Looking into the mirror, the tears I had been desperately trying to hold back fell down my face. I examined myself and ran a hand through my hair.

Why is this happening now? I'm finally getting myself together and learning to live without Karim, only for Nazir to blow back into my life. Why?

"I will kick this door down, and you know I will, Tatiana," Yaya's muffled voice threatened from the other side.

Wiping my tears, I opened the door, and she stepped inside, quickly closing it behind her.

"What's going on with you?"

"Nazir."

"Oh honey, I'm sorry. I know him coming back—"

"He was my driver this morning?"

She paused. "Is that in his job description?"

I plopped down on one of the cushioned benches. "Apparently, Jonah doesn't want anyone my father hired to work for me."

"I don't blame him. Anyone could be responsible for that hit on your father. What did he say that has you so emotional?"

"It's not about what he said. It's about him being here. I've held a mental funeral for this man, and then he just comes back from the dead."

I slammed my hand onto the granite—a little too hard because I felt the sting. But the pain in my hand didn't matter. All I wanted was for my heart to calm and my eyes to stop watering at the sight of that man. I longed for life to go back to how it was before he appeared downstairs in my home. Life wasn't great, but I was getting through it—faking it until I made it—and focusing on my daughter's happiness.

"Maybe this is God giving you what you asked for."

I turned and looked at her as if she had just cursed at me. "What?"

"I remember you crying when Karim passed. You said how every man you love leaves you. We were both drinking, but you were more drunk than I was."

As she jogged my memory, I started to remember that night. We were sitting out back while Nazira was asleep on my lap. Karim had been gone for two weeks, and I didn't want her away from me. During those first three nights after Karim's death, she woke up screaming for him. I would've done anything to erase her pain. If she wanted candy for dinner, I gave it to her because I didn't want her to hurt like I was.

"What does that have to do with anything?"

"You mentioned Nazir. Said you wished you could have that closure from him…that if he never left you, you wouldn't have to deal with the heartache."

I slapped my hand over my face and sighed. "It was the liquor talking."

"Drunk thoughts speak sober words. You've always wondered what happened to him, Tatiana. He's appeared again for a reason, and you need to find out what that reason is."

I snatched my bag from the counter and swung it onto my arm. "He came back to protect my family because that's what Jonah hired him to do. Nothing more."

She followed behind me into the locker room, where I aggressively shoved my bag into the locker after taking out my headphones.

"Then why are you so triggered by him?"

"Yaya, that man left me after promising forever. He never contacted me or came back for me. Seeing him triggers me because I'm reminded of the pain I went through."

She leaned against the locker, giving me an intense look. Whenever she stared at me like that, she always got me to admit what I was truly feeling—things I swore I'd take to the grave.

"I'm not saying you need to jump into bed with the man, but at least hear him out. How do you know leaving was an easy decision for him, Tatiana?"

"I don't care if it was hard. He should have told me instead of disappearing in the middle of the night. We told each other everything," I snapped, slamming the locker shut.

The entire morning had me off my game. I usually looked forward to working out, but now I didn't want to.

"Nazir is, what? A few years older than you?"

"Seven."

I remember lying to him about my age, claiming I was twenty-five. Nazir carried himself differently, and I could tell he was older than me. I didn't want him to dismiss me like I was some young, naïve college girl with a crush. I needed him to take me seriously, so yes, I lied about my age. Was I proud of that? No.

Eventually I came clean, and he laughed, saying I set him up. Being an only child, I've always been mature for my age. Did I want to date a man who was closer to my father's age than mine? Not really. However, I appreciated Nazir's maturity, wisdom, and conversation. We would become so lost in conversation that we'd lose track of time. I loved that our relationship was more than just sex. He was my first love—the first man I gave my heart to—and he broke it without having the balls to do it face to face.

"Maybe he didn't think you could handle the conversation. I mean, you're acting pretty immature right now."

I turned to curse her ass out and saw her grin. "Yaya, not today."

She followed me onto the gym floor, where our trainer was waiting. He was already on the phone and gesturing toward the stair stepper—we knew what to do.

"You said you never got the closure you needed, and now it's literally in your face. Yet, you don't want it."

"I have made peace with not knowing."

I began climbing the gruesome stairs, happy for the distraction. Yaya increased her speed— as she often did—and then looked over at me.

"If you've truly made peace, you wouldn't be as bothered as you are right now. Tatiana, I know you, and even though you've moved on, tell me you don't think about him sometimes. I'm not saying every day, but over the years, that man has crossed your mind."

"It's kind of hard not to think of him when I'm raising his child," I said, hanging my head and gripping the rails as I slowly climbed the moving stairs. "Every smile and facial expression makes me think of him."

"Which is exactly why you need to have that conversation with him."

"Negative."

"You plan to lie to Nazira her whole life? Let her believe one man was her father when her real father is very much alive?"

I did one full flight before turning my attention back to my best friend.

"Her father is in the ground. Karim may not have been her biological father, but he was there and stepped up to raise a child that wasn't his."

"Which I commend him for. Not many men would have done that. But you need to think of Nazir and how he would want to know about his daughter."

"Then he should've fucking stayed around," I said, then pulled my headphones over my ears, not wanting to hear anything else about this conversation.

I don't know why Yaya expected me to be the bigger person. He didn't care about us having a child when he left. Even without him knowing I was pregnant, he knew there was always the possibility I could get pregnant, especially with him having unprotected sex with me.

The bottom line is, Nazir left without ever checking on me. So, I don't think I wanted to know his reasons for doing what he did. Yeah, Yaya might think it was unfair of me to only acknowledge my hurt without knowing his reason for hurting me, but I didn't care.

At least...not yet.

After pacing my bedroom for an hour last night, I finally gave in and took one of my Ambien pills. My doctor prescribed them after diagnosing me with insomnia. I was hesitant to depend on medication for sleep because I worried I might become addicted. My eyes burned, my thoughts were foggy, and I accidentally sent an email to the CEO of Valora Hotels instead of Yaya. If there was ever a night I needed sleep, last night was it. I just wanted my mind to quiet down for a few hours.

Once I took the medicine, I went to Nazira's bedroom and quietly gathered up clothes and toys while she slept peacefully. After yawning for the fourth time in six minutes, I abandoned the mission and dragged myself to bed. With my eye mask on, I closed my eyes and didn't wake up until my alarm went off beside me. I can't say I felt fully refreshed, but I was no longer tired, and my head no longer ached from lack of sleep. That felt like a small victory.

I swung my legs out of bed and stood up to start my day. I went into the closet and tossed a dress I had been thinking about earlier this week into my open suitcase. My schedule was packed with meetings this week, so I decided to stay in the city. If that wasn't enough, I had to fly to Las Vegas this weekend for a meeting at the Valora Hotel. I hated traveling for work. Karim usually handled all the traveling when it came to Hush. He was the one who had been working on most of these deals, while I worked at the spa and made it home each night to be with our daughter.

As much as I loved being an entrepreneur, which could be very demanding at times, I also wanted to be present for Nazira. I wanted to be the mother who baked cookies and was always home when she got in from school. Now that it was just me, I couldn't be that mother anymore. Although I wasn't always home when she returned from school, I made sure to spend quality time with her and pour into her. Our cherished moments together brought me joy because I loved being with my child. Nazira was an amazing girl, and I felt pride whenever I looked into her eyes.

There were times when I felt guilty that Nazir missed her most important moments. For every first I shared with Karim, tears often fell when I was alone. I had been mourning for a long time, and then life took my husband, deepening my grief. I mourned every moment Nazir missed with our daughter, every moment we didn't get to experience together, and every promise he broke. Then, the mourning always stopped, and anger took its place.

The timing of this business trip was perfect since Aja was taking Nazira away for the weekend. Her niece had just turned ten and was having a birthday party, so she was taking Nazira with her.

My village always showed up for me and Nazira. I never had to ask for anything because they were always there to make sure we were taken care of. After finishing my morning bathroom routine, I shuffled back into my bedroom. Zira, sitting on the bed's edge, surprised me because I usually had to pry the girl out of bed in the mornings.

"Good morning, Mommy," she yawned.

I held my arms out, and she abandoned the bed to hug me. I kissed her head and looked down at her.

"Why are you awake so early?" I asked.

"I wanted to see you before you left for the city."

I smiled. "Baby, I was going to come and peek in on you. I can never leave without giving you a kiss."

She giggled as I tickled her. "Yeah, well, I'm never really awake–awake when you do."

"Very true. I'm going to miss you, but Bloom has everything under control," I assured her.

Bloom and I had gone over the schedule so many times that Emilio could recite each activity Nazira had without looking at the digital board in the kitchen.

"I know. Mommy, you've traveled for work before. I'm just gonna miss you because I'll be gone with Aja."

I hugged her a little tighter. "I know. I have a surprise for you when you come back."

At the mention of a surprise, she lit up. "What?"

"I'm taking you on my next business trip. I think some work and play balance is needed for both of us, right?"

She excitedly jumped up and down in excitement because she had never been on a business trip with me before.

Since we're expanding to the Dominican Republic soon, I wanted to make sure the resort was perfect for a Hush location. Hush focused on pampering women, especially mothers. I wanted to make sure that after a busy day of running after the kids at the resort, moms could enjoy being pampered by a highly certified staff.

"Yessss! Where are we going? Out the country? Out the world?"

I smiled as I listened to her giggle. I loved it when she acted silly. Being silly and carefree is part of being a child, but she didn't do it often. I didn't want her to feel like she had to be strong for me. I'm the parent, and she's the child. She shouldn't worry about her mother. It was my job to care for and protect her, not the other way around.

"I have an important business trip by the beach. While I work during the day, you can play on the beach with Bloom. Then, later, I'll join you—just us for dinner."

Her smile showed this was what she had wanted from me—us enjoying each other's time together.

"Is Yaya coming, too?"

"She'll be there, but mostly, it will be just you and me. Okay?"

"Sounds like the best idea, Mommy."

I kissed her nose, smiled, and said, "The greatest idea in the world. Love you, baby."

"Love you, too, Mommy."

I glanced at the clock. "Hmm, you still have an hour to get some sleep before getting up for school. Want to sleep in my bed?"

She looked around my room and shook her head no.

"You leave too many lights on. As long as I get my favorite hug, I can go back to my room."

I snuggled her one last time before she headed back down the hall to her bedroom. Glancing at the time again, I quickly packed my things, knowing I wouldn't have time to return to Greenwich if I forgot something.

"Dammit…you're not even that heavy," I muttered, struggling down the stairs with my carry-on luggage.

That familiar smell consumed me as I sensed a presence behind me.

"I got you."

Because I had been struggling since the top of the spiraled stairs, I allowed his hand to brush past me and grab the suitcase. I hurried down the remaining steps while he lifted my suitcase as if it were as light as doll furniture.

"Thanks. You can leave it at the front for the driver." I paused and turned around. "Unless you're the driver today."

He watched as I stood with my hand on my wide hip and took him in. He was wearing a gray Nike sweatsuit, and my eyes were having a hard time trying to avoid looking at his print. It was like he was deliberately teasing me by wearing sweats to work.

"Nah, everything checked out with your original driver, so he's back."

I squinted my eyes at him. Ralph had always been trustworthy and reliable since the day he started working for the Sterling family. Although my father was the one who hired him, he had always been like family.

"Did anyone even suspect Ralph of anything?"

He snorted. "Ralph needed the day off, and I filled in for him. What can I say—I'm always looking to help out anybody who needs it."

"Are sweats suitable work attire?" I replied sharply, making sure my tone sounded judgmental with each word.

He finally set the suitcase down. "I thought I'd come by and check on how things are going with Emilio."

"Well, Emilio runs a tight ship with his team, and he wouldn't approve of sweatpants. Why would you need to check in on your bos—"

"Good morning, boss. You didn't tell me you were coming by this morning."

Emilio extended his hand, and I watched as the two dapped each other.

"I was in the area and figured I would escort Mrs. Sterling to the city…keep some of you here."

"Good look. Let me know if you need anything."

I glanced between Emilio and Nazir. They paid me no mind as they continued their conversation. Instead of standing there with my foot in my mouth, I turned and went to the kitchen to fill my water bottle and grab some snacks. The drive to the city was only about an hour, so I planned to get some work done and snack on rice crackers during the ride. As I filled my water bottle, I heard those flat feet splatting across the marble floor.

"Mom!"

She often switched between calling me mom or mommy. I preferred mommy because that meant she was still my little button and not growing up on me.

"Yes, baby?"

I peered from the kitchen as Nazir looked at her.

"How are you doing? It's nice to meet you, again." Nazir was entirely focused on our daughter—a daughter he didn't know he had.

"Good morning, sir."

He chuckled. "My name is Nazir, but you can call me Naz."

I heard Nazira gasp, and I quickly jerked my head back inside the kitchen, resting it on the fridge. Since he had been around, we had only called her Zira. Now he was about to find out just how much we shared together.

"My name is Nazira! Mommy, did you hear his name?"

I swallowed the lump threatening to jump out of my throat and looked nervously back out.

"Uh-huh. What are the odds?" I replied.

Nazir stared at me, communicating silently. He was hurting, but not because of me. He was hurting because he left us.

"You're going to be seeing a lot of me around, *Name Twin*."

"To keep me and mommy safe, right?"

He smiled as he looked down at her, then his eyes met mine again.

"Yes, I'm going to keep you and your mother safe. I'm not going anywhere again."

I popped my head back into the kitchen while holding my chest. It wasn't that I was expecting her to never say her full name around him. Oh, hell! Who was I kidding? That's exactly what my delusional ass was hoping. Ever since security started staying at the house, Nazir hadn't been around much—aside from when he took on the role of driver. I didn't realize he owned the security company, which probably explained his distance. He didn't have to be here because he had staff handling the work.

Taking a few deep breaths, I heard those slaps of feet on the marble again and managed to put on a smile, even though I felt the opposite at the time. Nazira rounded the corner and held up the charm bracelet she had made for me. She never let me travel without it, and I had forgotten to grab it while doing a million things.

"My girl," I said with a smile, taking the bracelet and quickly clasping it around my wrist. "What would I do without you, Nazira?"

"Forget your favorite bracelet," she replied, chuckling. "Have a safe trip, Mommy."

I kissed her cheeks. "Thanks, babe. Now go get some more sleep and call me when you're awake and heading to school."

"Okay," she said, then skipped back toward the stairs where Nazir stood.

"Don't forget, lil lady."

She grinned—the same one she shared with the man standing behind her. "I promise I won't forget."

"Okay."

Once she disappeared up the stairs, I continued to busy myself in the kitchen.

"Tata," his deep voice called from behind me.

I had no choice but to ignore him because what would I say? How could I tell him that Nazira was his daughter? She resembled him, and from the way he studied her since the moment he met her, he already knew it.

"Are my bags in the car? I don't want to run into traffic this morning," I quickly replied, hoping to avoid the conversation I knew he wanted to have.

I didn't want to talk about it right now. Or ever. I knew I would get too emotional, and I didn't need that at this moment. I refused to let him knock me off my square another morning. I had meetings today, and I needed to be focused.

"I don't want to talk about the fucking bags, Tatiana."

I spun around on my heels, keeping my posture straight and thoughts calm.

"And I don't care to discuss whatever is swirling in your brain. Please make sure my car is ready to go, Mr. Kane."

"Tat—"

"Mrs. Sterling," I corrected him, then left out the kitchen.

I quickly ducked into one of the powder rooms and took a few deep breaths. This wasn't my fault. Hell, I didn't run away from him. He was the one who left me. So why did I feel so guilty?

After spending thirty minutes on my makeup, I made sure not to splash water on my face. Staring into the mirror, I removed a stray hair from my face and pressed my hand to my chest while silently counting down from twenty. Once my heart steadied, I walked out of the bathroom and headed toward the front. As I came down the hall, Bloom shuffled down the stairs with a blanket wrapped around her shoulders, her hair matted to her head, and dried drool and last night's makeup still on her face.

None of that mattered to Emilio, though, as he smiled at her. "Good morning, Bloom."

She snapped out of her zombie-like trance and offered him a smile. "Too early to be speaking, Emmy."

"Emilio, beloved," he said, correcting her.

She yawned. "Too early to be getting names correct, too."

I watched as she pulled the covers tighter around her arms and walked toward me.

"Safe drive into the city. Everything here is handled, so you don't need to worry or call a million times."

"Aja will be picking her up from school on Friday, so you have the weekend free," I told her.

She shrugged while walking to the fridge. "Not like I have much of a life anyway. I'll either be here or at my loft asleep."

Once I gave Bloom the rundown again, I finally stepped out of the house and got into the black SUV that would take me to the city. Ralph was back in his rightful place as my driver, and all was good in the world. That was until the door on the opposite side of me opened, and Nazir stepped his tall ass into the back with me.

"Um, what are you doing?"

"Security, Mrs. Sterling," he smartly replied as he checked his watch and nodded at Ralph to go.

As Ralph pulled out of the gates, I stared at Nazir as if he might suddenly jump out of the car. I actually wished he would jump out while it was moving because I knew sitting in the car with him for an hour would be unbearable. I rummaged through my purse and pulled out my headphones because the last thing I wanted was to hear the awkward silence between us. He stared at me for a few moments, but when I didn't make eye contact, he turned his attention out the window.

As soon as we hit the city, I was on the go with different meetings. We were launching new products in the spa, and we wanted to ensure the formula remained clean, as Yaya had requested. She was obsessed with having products that did more good than harm. Everything, from the bottles to the formula, was green and clean. The bottles were made of recycled glass, and we always encouraged people on our social media platforms to reuse the glass from our products. Yaya had suggested offering refillable options so the bottles could be used more than once, which I thought was a great idea.

While it was nice having my best friend as both a business partner and my assistant, I had been telling Yaya to find her replacement for a year, but she refused. She claimed no one could do what she does for me. That may have been true, but I often felt guilty for relying so heavily on her. Even with me tossing anything her way, she was capable of handling it because she always got it done.

Nazir had been with me the entire day, doing his job and offering no conversation. I appreciated that. I already had a lot that I was dealing with today and didn't want him following me around and begging to have a conversation.

He held the door open as I entered what would become the second Hush location. Our realtor, who was currently out of town, had given us the code so we could tour the place.

"This is perfect. I feel so calm just walking into the space," I said out loud, while Yaya followed behind me.

"I'm thinking we can add some walls there to block the view to the back. Being that this used to be a boutique hotel, we can utilize so much. The plunge pools can be down here on the main floor toward the back, and the infinity pool on the rooftop is perfect," Yaya suggested.

Her excitement made me even more excited because I could see our vision right in front of us. It would take some time to get everything how we wanted it, but once everything was done, it would be perfect.

It also gave me an excuse to delay telling Karim's mother and mine that I would be moving myself and Nazira to the city. Nazira would adapt, and our family could always visit when they missed us. It was only an hour away, not twenty. Being in the city had always made me feel alive, and I had stayed away for too long, only experiencing it in doses. Losing Karim reminded me how short life is, and I refused to sit and not do what I wanted.

"We need to move fast and make an offer. Somebody will snatch this up quickly."

"It's a miracle he hasn't received an offer yet," Yaya said as she sat down on a piece of furniture left behind. "You think we can negotiate these chairs? They're quite cute and expensive, too."

When Nazir stepped outside to join the other security guard, I whispered to Yaya, "He found out about Nazira."

"I'm not surprised," she replied casually.

"Why do you say you're not surprised?"

She crossed her legs. "Pictures didn't do him justice. In person, I can see Nazira in him. That little grin she does? He does the same one— been doing it all day whenever you walk into a room."

"Really? Never mind." I stopped myself from blushing.

Yaya laughed. "How did that conversation go?"

"What conversation?"

She stared at me, confused. "You didn't have a conversation with him about it?"

I stood up and walked behind the front desk. "No."

"Why not?"

"It was chaotic this morning, and I didn't need to be in my feelings. Plus, I haven't even fully processed how I feel my damn self, Yalina."

Yaya held her hands up. "Relax. I'm just asking."

"Do I even have to tell her? It's one thing for us to know because we're her parents. Does she really need to know?"

"Tatiana, she needs to know. As much as you don't want to have this talk with her, this is also her life. You don't have the right to keep that from her."

"She's too young to go through all of this," I whined, stomping my feet.

Yaya's phone rang, and she quickly silenced it. "I'm not in the mood to deal with her today."

"What did she do now?"

"I'm tired of it always being the Sav show. Everyone's wronged her, and she's never at fault. Sick of hearing how I'm doing everything wrong."

I noticed the worn expression cross my best friend's face. The only time I saw this expression was when she talked about Sav. Yaya wasn't happy with her before she was locked up, and now she was really miserable in their relationship. Honestly, I never understood why she wanted to be with her. Sav was unpleasant to be around—always suspicious, confrontational, and full of jealousy. I always wondered how Yalina put up with her.

Stress clouded her eyes. "Your birthday is this weekend. It's bad enough you're forcing us to go on this business trip during it. Don't let her ruin this week and weekend for you. Block her until next week."

She looked up at me. "Do you know the hysteria it would cause with her? She'll claim it was an emergency because I didn't answer."

I came from around the counter, gently took her phone, and silenced the incoming call. I then checked her call log, blocked the prison's number, and returned the phone back to her.

"Sav's emergency isn't your emergency. I think you tell yourself that you're going to break up when she comes home, but we both know you're going to stay. Sav will convince you that she's going to change, and you'll stay where everything feels familiar."

"Not you clocking my tea. You need to mind your business and worry about that fine-ass man you need to remember how to climb."

I playfully shoved her and plopped down in the chair next to her while we laughed.

"Girl, those sweatpants had me forgetting why I was so angry with him."

Yaya chuckled. "You used to take that, huh? I can see why you were so mad when you had to marry Karim."

I burst into laughter. "Bitch, too damn soon."

Yaya laughed. "All I'm saying is that we both find ourselves in situations. Yours isn't as bad. If I were you, I'd be fucking the shit out of the ghost from my past. Would've jumped on him like, 'Bust me down, baby!'"

"Yalina Blackwell!" I howled at her.

Just then, Nazir swaggered back through the door.

"Like the space?" he asked.

"It's perfect," Yaya replied.

"Seems nice." He stood in front of us with his hands in his pockets. "Where to next?"

"This was the last thing on our jam-packed schedule. It wasn't too bad, huh?" she joked with him.

He smirked. "Nah. Actually inspiring to see two women holding it down. I'm proud of you, Tata."

Yaya raised her eyebrows. "Tata? Hmm."

"Yalina, please," I rolled my eyes and waved her off.

She laughed. "Anyway, I have some last-minute shopping to do, so me and Smoke will be going to do that."

Jonah was serious about keeping us all safe. Just like Nazira and I had our own guards, Yaya had the same. He knew she was independent and wouldn't want to stay at his house long-term, so he made sure she had her own protection. Yaya was accustomed to doing everything herself, never relying on anyone to take care of her. She was the person who took care of everyone.

"Yeah, you go and do that."

She giggled as she stood up and kissed my cheek. "I'll email the realtor tonight to let him know we want to move forward with making an offer. I'm sure we can get the price down some."

I watched as she switched toward the door, her heels clicking loudly on the floor.

"Love you, Ya."

"Love you, too. Call me later."

"Will do."

I stayed seated after she left and finally got the courage to look into Nazir's eyes.

"Tata, we need to tal—"

Before he could finish, I hopped up and headed to the front desk to grab my purse. "As much as you want to sit and talk, I'm not there yet."

"Not about where you are with us—it's about my daughter."

"You don't know that she's your daughter."

He tilted his head, staring down into my eyes. "You gonna lie that easy?"

I swung my purse onto my arm and started walking toward the door. "Can we go?"

He nodded and caught up to step in front of me, pulling me behind him. Once we reached the car, he held the door open for me. I settled into the seat and closed my eyes.

Why me, Lord?

CHAPTER TEN

Tatiana

I FELT SICK *to my stomach as I looked over myself in the mirror.*

Today was my wedding day and I was getting married to someone that I didn't know. Every time I brought it up, my mother or father would remind me that we went to middle school together. Middle school was ages ago, and it wasn't something that I really never remembered.

If Karin Sterling was someone I was supposed to know and marry, then I would have remembered him. I would have run into his arms and been excited to walk down the aisle to him. Instead, I felt this lump in my throat, and wave of sickness in my stomach. My body was telling me to run away and not go through with this.

As much as I wanted to listen to my body, I also knew that I couldn't. My father had gone through so much for this wedding and for our marriage. Apparently, it was a union that was always supposed to happen.

The door creaked and I saw my father coming into the room. The photographer followed him as he smiled with this look of pride on his face, taking in the dress that I wore. It was flown in from Italy. A mermaid style dress with beautiful lace flowers that were sewn one by one onto the dress.

My veil floated behind me as I walked with the Sterling crest embroider into the lace. As sad as I was today, I couldn't deny that I felt beautiful in this dress. The only thing that I kept thinking about was Nazir. How much I wanted it to be him that I was coming down the aisle to.

"Tati, you look beautiful, Baby… like an angel," he came and gave me a kiss on both of my cheeks, as he looked down at me.

The photographers took pictures of us having our first look as father and daughter. My father quickly dismissed him once he finished doing his bow for the photos.

I dropped my smile as I returned back to looking in the mirror. My father looked from behind me as I messed with my hands. In this moment I was resentful of my father. Resenting the life that I could have had. Instead of being seconds away from walking down the aisle, I could have been enjoying college and having fun.

Have love with the love of my life, not sitting here about to vow to love someone that I didn't even love. How did my mother do this?

"Moving up the wedding date was the smartest thing to do." He said, from behind me, as I avoided eye contact with him.

I was supposed to have months to prepare for this, and it was slapped right into my face. Forcing me to deal with what I never wanted to deal with in the first place. Instead of being a father, he was treating me like a cash cow. Stock that he could just use whenever he wanted.

"Why do I have to do this?" My voice broke, hoping that he would find it in his heart to just love me.

Be my father and not the businessman he had always been. I wanted him to protect me because that was something he had never done before. Instead, he looked at me in the eyes, fixing a loose strand of hair from my updo before smiling.

"Ruin this, Tatiana, and I'll make sure that you won't be able to fucking speak through your wired jaw."

I gasped, as he walked away and then turned back around. "I hate you."

He chuckled. "Tati, I'm not someone to love… I was born not to be loved… as your father, this is the plan, and I don't want to hear shit else."

He opened the door, and did a fake ass hearty laugh like we were having a good time in here. I looked at the door and all I saw was hate for a man that was supposed to my father. How could my mother love him?

She was just as unhappy and now I was forced to be the same. Forced to marry and love a man that I wasn't in love with, or knew. Karim could have been a great guy, but I didn't know him.

The door opened once more and my mother stood there. She paused and took in everything that I had on, holding back tears like this was a happy moment. As if I was marrying the love of my life and wasn't being forced.

"Why are you so happy about me marrying a man I don't know?" I muttered.

She walked across the room and put her arms around me, both of us staring into the mirror. "Right now, none of this makes sense… I know. I always want you happy and taken care of, and this secures that. Baby, there's so much you don't know, but I know one thing, those Sterlings will protect you."

"Mom, what are you not saying?"

She kissed my cheek gently. "I was here before… here because my father thought this was best. I can promise you the best thing that happened out of all of this is you, Tatiana. You are my entire world."

"Mom, please."

"I would run away with you, baby, I would, but your father. Just do as he says and I promise we won't suffer for much longer." She squeezed me, and then looked over me once more.

My mother loved being my mother, and as she started at me, I could tell she loved me. Unlike my father, he looked me over like a prized horse in a show. One that would secure him even more money.

"Now, you go down that aisle and put the best show on... I promise, Tati...the Sterlings are good people." She assured me again, as if she knew something that I didn't know.

That lump never disappeared, but I somehow felt a bit better. A bit softer, and ready to get this over with. Would I make it easy on my new husband?

Absolutely not.

CHAPTER ELEVEN

Jonah

THERE WAS NOTHING worse than your ass itching in public. You couldn't scratch it because people would start judging like their own asses had never itched before. Then niggas would assume you were dirty because your ass was itching. Like the cleanest muthafuckas didn't get a slight itch now and then. Either way, your ass itching in public was the worst thing that could happen. Something you despised, even though it didn't happen often.

That was how I felt about Malcolm Rich. That nigga made my ass itch in the worst way. Everything about him screamed snake, but I always had to play it cool because Karim told me that was family.

I knew he started to fall in love with Tatiana when he began trying to protect Malcolm. When his father first told him he had to marry her, he wasn't with that shit. He wanted to find some blackmail or something to try and convince his father not to fuck with Malcolm. Then, he met Tatiana, and all that talk went out the window.

Karim was someone who cared about those around him. It started to make sense the more I got to know Tatiana myself. Her own father never protected her like a father should. Instead, he pushed her to marry into a family and forced her to give up her own life. That's the reason Karim was so protective of her.

Then Tatiana had Nazira, and his entire world changed. Everything was about his family, and for the first time, I saw my best friend genuinely happy. Not that fake-ass happy, but the kind that felt so good others caught second-hand happiness from it.

That happiness from my memories faded the minute I pulled into the long-gated driveway in Long Island. Malcolm's dusty ass had been hiding in Long Island ever since someone tried to pop his top. I was doing everything I could to make sure Tatiana and Nazira were safe. Whoever tried to get at him, I knew he deserved whatever was coming. Trouble found that man because he was trouble.

The thing about doing dirt is that you eventually have to lay down in it. We all did shit that we weren't proud of, but a day comes when you have to answer for it. Someone was trying to put that man in the dirt, and he wasn't going to take my sister and goddaughter with him.

"Ma, nobody can make sausage and peppers like you do," I said between chews of the best sausage and peppers I'd ever had.

No matter how many times I had Carlotta's sausage and peppers, they always got better each time. She smiled as she wiped her hands on the dish towel and came back over to where I was enjoying the feast.

Carlotta was Italian—an old-school Italian. You didn't visit without leaving with a full stomach and plastic containers filled with food. Even though she didn't know I was going to show up today, she still had food ready for me.

As soon as I stepped through the door, she hugged me and headed straight for the fridge to pull out the leftovers she'd cooked. Tatiana didn't come over often, and after losing both Karim and Raphael, she was left alone. But that didn't stop her from cooking like they were still here. I knew those niggas from Nazir's security team were eating good.

"Nobody better make you sausage and peppers. Only Mama," she said, then kissed my head.

Her thick Queens accent was one of my favorite things about her. It didn't matter how long she had been in high society or how much money she had; she never cared to bow down to what society expected from her. She kept her thick Howard Beach accent.

"How have you been, Ma? You know I can find you a condo closer to me. This house is too big for just you," I said.

She continued to wipe her hands on the dish towel, then flipped it over her shoulder. I watched as her diamond and pearl earrings shimmered in the sunlight coming through the kitchen window.

"This is my home, Jonah. I can't leave my home," she replied, leaning on the counter with a sigh.

I cut into the eggplant parmesan she had set on the counter. "I worry about you, Ma."

Carlotta Sterling wasn't just Karim's mother; she was also mine and had accepted me as her own. From the day her son came home talking about a friend he met at a charity event; she never looked down on me.

I met Karim when he attended a charity event his father was involved in. He was standing off to the side while I sat on the steps nearby. Even back then, I hated being pitied. I wasn't a charity case, but you couldn't tell that to my mother. She was being honored for her contribution as a foster mother. My mother never turned away a child, making our home crowded and chaotic.

While she focused on giving other children love, her biological child was often overlooked in the shuffle of new children coming in and out. She even adopted some. Our home was like a fucking pound for abandoned kids.

I went from having my own room to sharing it with three other boys. Nothing was mine anymore, and I never got my mother's attention. Whenever I voiced wanting to spend time with her, she would remind me of how fortunate we were to be able to help other children in need of love.

At times, I looked at her and wanted to yell, "Fuck them kids." I needed her, but she was so caught up in the high she got from helping people. My mother was one of those who got a high from doing good for others—so much so that she started neglecting herself.

When I met Karim, we clicked instantly. I could tell from his shiny dress shoes and miniature tie that matched his father's tie that he wasn't from around my way. No sooner was he away from his Au pair and father, the good boy act dropped, and I saw the little wannabe hoodlum.

He might have had a silver spoon shoved in his mouth, but the boy was dying to pull it out, put that bitch on a scale, and break it down to sell.

When he left the event that day, I just knew I wouldn't see him again. The center where the ceremony took place was a place I spent a lot of time. My mother was always volunteering, and it was somewhere she could take us kids to burn off the energy she was always talking about.

I always knew I wanted more than what I had been handed. My mother wasn't rich by any means, but she still gave her last to help those in need. Her sacrifice wasn't just hers; it was mine, too. I was the one who went without since we couldn't afford to do it. The problem was, we could have afforded it if she hadn't kept taking in more mouths to feed. School field trips, new sneakers, and just a second helping of dinner were always denied. I was made to feel selfish because I wanted more.

Fuck that.

I never asked to be brought into this world, so the small shit I was asking for as a kid, I should've been able to get that shit. It made me hate others because I was the one getting the short end of the stick. My mother had always been an unkept woman, always giving everyone her all when she had very little for herself. She taught me a valuable lesson at a young age.

Growing up, the streets were all I knew. If I wanted better for myself, I knew I had to get it out the mud. Having a friend who could snap his fingers and get whatever he wanted was inspiring. I wanted to build a life like that for myself, and I didn't want any help doing it.

It wasn't until I was older that I learned that the long money the Sterlings had wasn't all legal. Raphael had his hands in a little bit of everything, and at one point, our hands were in the same jar. When he realized what I was doing, he brought me onto his team, and it's been up ever since. Raphael treated me like his second son and knew my loyalty toward him and his family was solid. It was the reason Carlotta would always be taken care of; I would make sure of it.

"Eat more." She pushed the bruschetta toward me. "I have the security, and they keep me safe. I go and visit the spa when I need to get out. Tatiana makes sure the girls treat me nice, eh."

"It doesn't help me worry any less. I hate you being in this big house. Karim would hate it, too."

She paused for a moment, then leaned on the counter. "He would hate you worrying about me. Do I miss my husband? Sureee," she said, dragging out her words. "But he was sick."

Instead of harping on things that neither of us could control, I continued to eat my food.

"What do you get into being in this big house?"

"Read and cook. Malcolm came by to check on me. God bless him."

I tried to hide my disgust because she was excited he had come to visit. But I knew Malcolm didn't give a fuck about Raphael when he was sick. The nigga didn't even attend the funeral. He gave some bullshit-ass excuse about why he couldn't make it.

"Oh yeah?"

"He declined food, but we sat on the back patio and had some tea. Told me that he broke up with his girlfriend—you know, the one he got with after his divorce."

"He's a rich Black man. I'm sure he has plenty of women to keep him company."

Carlotta smiled and shrugged. "Should have never let his wife leave him. Men like Raphael and Malcolm need strong women by their sides. I was by Raphael's side until his last days."

"And he loved you till the very end."

My guard was up when I heard Malcolm had come to visit Carlotta. Malcolm wasn't the type to just come and shoot the breeze with you. If he came to see you, it was because he wanted something. I couldn't think of what he could possibly want from Carlotta.

"I want you to find a love like Raphael and I had, Jo. You need to settle down with a good girl and have some children."

I washed down my food with my water. "I don't think love is in the cards for me, Ma."

As much as I craved finding real love—the kind that would make me want to let down my walls, the shit also terrified me. I wanted Yalina Blackwell, and she knew it. The only reason I tolerated the cat-and-mouse games we played with each other was because I was scared of her. Yalina had the power to make me break down these walls and let her in. There hadn't been a woman who had been able to make me fall in love. I mean, they were cool to slut out and shit, but none of them made me want to slide a ring onto their finger. Yalina did. I wanted to give her the dream life—a life where she could be carefree because she knew her man had shit covered.

"Love is for everyone. I keep telling Tatiana that she will find love again, but she doesn't want to hear it. Maybe it's why she doesn't come over often anymore," she chuckled.

"She's just trying to find her way since losing Karim. I know coming over here is hard because everything here reminds her of him."

She rubbed my arm. "I'm teasing with you. I know Tatiana is trying to find her way without Karim. As his mother, even I know it's time for her to move forward. Karim would want the same for her."

I kissed her hand. "We love you, Ma. Never forget that."

She pinched my cheeks. "I know it and can't ever forget it."

Carlotta checked on me more than my own mother did. I got maybe three calls a year from my birth mother, and that was usually when money's low. She was too busy helping and being everything to everyone else.

My adoptive sister had about six kids and lived off my mom. Bitch was lazy and always found ways to milk the system and take advantage of my mother. You would think she would want to focus on taking care of the damn kids she already had, but instead she laid on her nasty back and had more. Always talking about I'm their uncle. Fuck them kids. I didn't know their asses, and I kept my distance because she wasn't related to me.

After spending time with Carlotta, I kissed her cheek and headed out. As long as she was good, I was good.

***Macy:** I'm home if you want to slide through.*

I looked at my phone as I climbed into my truck, smirking at the text I received.

***Me:** On my way.*

My fist collided with the nigga's face in front of me, and he dropped to the floor. He then curled up into the fetal position as I commenced to whipping his ass. All that could be heard throughout the warehouse were grunts and cries of agony as I kept pounding on him. When I finished, I spat on him before stepping back to admire my work. His pussy ass was lying on the ground, whimpering like a pussy while I stared down at him in disgust.

"Stealing from me when I'm the most generous nigga there is. Every time you came to me about some bread, I looked out for you."

I grunted as I kicked him again, and he let out a loud squeal like a pig on a farm.

It didn't matter how much money I had invested in real estate, stocks, and businesses; there was nothing like street money. It was faster, abundant, and you didn't have a bunch of crackers in your face asking questions. It was powerful being in professional spaces with those assholes while knowing you had your hand in other things.

When people met Raphael Sterling, they assumed he made his money legally, and that was true. But there was another side of him that I witnessed—one that wasn't the Raphael who played golf at the country club on weekends or the one who cracked rich laughs and used words like "alrighty". They never got to see the man who snapped a man's neck with his bare hands or waited early in the morning with his hands in his pockets, watching a shipment come into port. He was silent with his shit; you would never hear him throwing around his weight. People just knew he was about that life, and they respected it.

While Malcolm always had to be loud about his shit, Raphael was different. When you were about that shit, you never had to be loud and prove it. Niggas just knew or heard how you got down and didn't want to be a lesson.

Even with me working for Raphael, he made it so I could step out and do my own thing. He taught me how to fish, so I never had to depend on anyone, not even him. For that, my loyalty would always be to him, and it didn't matter that he was in the ground.

"Looks like you got some shit on your hands," Nazir said from behind me.

I kept my eyes on the nigga on the floor and kicked him in his ribs before turning around. As much as I wanted to pull the trigger, I couldn't because he was my so-called nephew. I didn't give a fuck about putting him on or trying to push him to do better. He wanted to be out in the streets, so I showed him a better way.

"Fucking stealing from me like I don't do enough around this bitch."

I heard somebody clear their throat. "Boss, he wasn't stealing. The nigga he put on been stealing," one of my little niggas said, correcting me.

I looked over at him and shook my head. "So, you just bringing thieves into the fold, Matthew?"

A few of them chuckled at me using his real name.

"This nigga's name Matthew? Dozer, why you ain't put us on?" one of them clowned.

He strutted around acting like he was the biggest and baddest but had brought a thief into my operation. It didn't matter that he wasn't directly involved; this was a lesson to remind him and anyone else who I was associated with that they needed to be solid. Clearly, his ass didn't do a streetfax on the nigga.

Nazir laughed as he took up space in the doorway. The nigga nearly had to duck to enter the room. I was roughly 6'3", but he even had me beat when it came to height. It wasn't just the height, either; the nigga had muscle and could probably crack a skull with one finger. I watched as he looked at all the other knuckleheads laughing, memorizing their faces in case they ever came in his circle again.

"Bring me that fucking friend. Why the fuck you ain't lead with that?" I said, mushing the one who hollered out the correct information.

He stood there solid, not cowering or falling down. "Got you. My fault, boss."

Ignoring him, I headed down the hall to one of the bullshit offices. This spot was out in Harlem and wasn't used often by us. I just happened to be in some pussy when I got the call. Since I was closer to this location than our main headquarters, I instructed my workers and Nazir to meet me there.

Banga, one of my right hands, hit me up and told me he had found out who was responsible for the missing money. I appointed Banga to be my right-hand man because he handled business. That nigga was like a brother to me. We grew up together, and he held me down throughout the years. After I bounced out of my mom's house, it was Banga who offered up his mama's couch for me. He didn't give a fuck that I was broke and just starting out; whatever he had—which wasn't much—was mine.

When Karim and his parents moved out of New York for a few years, I realized I needed to focus on myself. I wasn't about to sit back like a stray dog, hoping they would come back for me. It was me and Banga out there handling business and trying to come up. That nigga had my back, and I had his front. That's how it had always been. So, when the Sterlings moved back and Raphael put me on, I made sure Banga came along with me.

"I hope you didn't ask me to come to this shithole just to watch you beat children," Naz said, taking a seat in one of the chairs as I rounded the raggedy wooden desk.

Laughing, I flipped my middle finger at him. "Shut the fuck up. I asked yo' freakishly large ass out here because I need you to make some shit make sense for me."

He raised his brow. "Ight. What do you need me to make sense for you?"

From his tone, I could tell he already knew where I was heading with the conversation. When Nazir and Tatiana saw each other downstairs the day I hired him, I sensed there was something more between them than being just old friends. There was chemistry, and from the way she had been acting lately, everything was starting to make more sense. Not to mention my godbaby had the female version of his name. Nazira wasn't some common name that every woman was naming their daughters. That shit wasn't even on the baby name website. Trust me, I checked.

Yes, Tatiana was still my sister, but I knew there were parts of her life she kept secret or only shared with her confidante, Yalina. Yaya held all her secrets, some even Bloom didn't know. She was her safe space to vent, and after everything she'd been through, I couldn't blame her.

Yalina was the kind of woman who made you feel safe and secure. So, I could see why Tatiana felt comfortable sharing her deepest secrets with her. Yaya was so damn nurturing, and a nigga needed that in his life. Most often, the women who were the most nurturing were the ones who needed to be nurtured, and I wanted to be the one to do that for her. I wanted to be the man who got her to lower those walls and let me in. To give her good dick while reassuring her that I wasn't going anywhere.

"You and Tatiana."

He quietly laughed to himself. "She's a client."

"Yet, you haven't taken a single payment. Matter of fact, the wire payment was reversed back into my account."

"Not all of it."

"Yeah, the security for Yaya was kept."

Nazir leaned forward. "I'm not paying for protection for another man's woman. It's clear she means a lot to you for you to be dropping the amount of money you are on her."

"Stop talking in circles and let me know what the fuck is up? We go back a long way, Naz."

Naz and I grew up in the same hood, and there was always mutual respect between us. So, when it came to needing protection, I knew this nigga was the one I wanted to go with. I didn't need a bunch of uptight bitches who did things by the book. If some shit popped off, I needed to know the problem would be handled without involving the police. Naz and his security team would make sure of that.

"Why was the money returned, Naz?"

He clasped his hands together and rested them on his stomach. "I think you already know, Jonah."

"Stop fucking with me."

"I'm not going to charge to protect my daughter and the woman who should've been my wife."

It was one thing to suspect it; it was another to actually hear it come from his mouth. Even as I sat across from him, I could see Nazira all through his face. Karim not being Nazira's biological father wasn't a secret to me. I knew Nazira had a father out there. I just never imagined we would cross paths this way.

"Man to man, what's the story behind the two of you?"

He relaxed some, his hands dropping to the arms of the chair as he looked at me.

"She's the love of my life—the one I let get away. There hasn't been a woman who could compare since."

"If she's the love of your life, how the fuck or why the fuck would you let her get away?"

He chuckled, mostly to himself. "Back then, I was a fucking coward—weak and scared. I pretended to be a man, but when faced with real-men responsibilities, I got cold feet and ran. Tata was putting her life into my hands, and I was too scared to tell her the truth. I left her when she needed me. That's some sucka shit I can't forgive myself for. I hurt her, probably causing her trust issues now."

I admired him for his honesty and for taking accountability. Many men couldn't admit their mistakes or accept responsibility for the hurt they caused women, leaving pain etched in their hearts. It was never "Sorry because I fucked up," or "I hurt you, and I shouldn't have done that." Nah, they would rather gaslight and shift the blame to the woman. But here was Nazir—sitting in front of me and admitting his fault. I couldn't do anything but respect him for that.

"You think reappearing in her life is going to make things better for her?"

He calmly clasped his hands back together. "No. I think my presence causes her pain and makes her anxious."

This nigga was too damn honest. I was hoping he would've said that his coming back would make it better for Tatiana. Instead, he slapped my ass with a Uno reverse card and had me even more confused about how to respond.

"Naz, what the hell is your endgame? Tatiana and Nazira are family, and I'm here to protect them. They already lost my best friend, and she doesn't need some bullshit that's gonna make her want to turn to crack."

Nazir jerked his head back, confused by my statement. "The hell?"

"What I'm saying is I don't want her stressed out about some shit. Who says you won't run again?"

"'Cause I know I can take care of her. Back then, I was a broke twenty-eight-year-old fucking with a rich girl. I had her wanting to leave that life behind to be with me, and I couldn't handle that pressure. How the fuck was I going to take care of her?"

He had a point. As a man, I understood his perspective. Tatiana had always known wealth and never experienced life without it. She didn't know what struggle meals were or how to survive the winter without heat—just your stove on and the door open, hoping to warm the whole apartment. I loved her, but she didn't know shit about the hood. If Nazir had decided to run away with her, her life would have changed drastically.

"I hear you."

"I don't regret my decision."

I sighed. "Even knowing that she was pregnant with your daughter?"

He leaned forward again. "If I hadn't left and had brought her into my world, I would have done anything to make money to take care of her. I wouldn't have moved with precision and brains; it would have been more out of survival because I would've had not one, but two mouths to feed. The way I would've been out there, I know I would have landed in prison. And me landing in prison would have done what for her?"

"Shit."

"I don't regret leaving Tatiana because I felt I was protecting her. However, I regret not being there for her and not being able to be a father to my daughter," Nazir said softly, his voice quieter than before.

I leaned back in my chair, giving him the space to get it all out. Who was I to judge another man when my own shit wasn't perfect?

"Since seeing Nazira, that guilt has haunted the fuck out of me. Even after hurting Tatiana, she still named her after me. She still chose me during a time when I wasn't there for her. It hurts me because my daughter knows another man as her father."

"For what it's worth, he was good to her," I said, making sure he knew it. "I don't know how much that helps you, but Karim treated Tatiana and Nazira like gold."

Nazir nodded slowly while focusing on his hands. Still, I could tell that knowing this mattered to him. It may not have soothed the pain he felt, but it made him feel something.

"I know I can't undo all the pain that I caused Tata," he said, his voice rougher. "But I'm here, and I want to fix it. Do the work to earn her trust back and heal the heart I'm responsible for breaking."

This was a conversation he needed to have. I could tell from the way his hands clenched at his sides, as if he was trying to keep himself from falling apart.

"Nazira is my daughter," he said, meeting my gaze. "She looks just like my mother and her sister."

"It's not my place to speak on the decisions Tatiana has to make. I'm Nazira's godfather, and I love that little girl more than the moon and stars. I'm just here...supporting Tatiana in whatever she wants."

He slowly shook his head, as if he couldn't believe the universe was playing a part in him reuniting with his family. Something from his past, which had scared him before, had come back to him. Another chance for him to prove himself and show Tatiana he could be what she needed, not just financially.

"I want a chance to step up and be the man they both need."

His eyes locked with mine, and I reached across the table to give him a dap.

CHAPTER TWELVE

Nazir

"We Can't Be Friends" by Deborah Cox and R.L.

THERE WAS SOMETHING about the way God forced you to see the error of your ways. It was one thing to know it, and another to be reminded of it. He wanted to bring me to my knees so I could see just how royally I had fucked up with Tatiana. Not much could knock me off my square—except her.

After parking in front of the building, I sat there for a second with my hands on the steering wheel and my heart pounding. This building represented a person I hadn't encountered in years—someone I had lost contact with. This building had my heart smeared on its walls, all the way up to the twenty-first floor. It held things that neither Tatiana nor I ever spoke out loud. The memories were woven among the silk sheets and restless nights. It was our personal sanctuary, where we kept secrets we were too afraid to share with the outside world.

The valet attendant stood at the entrance, unsure whether he should come to get my keys or remain there, waiting for me to emerge from behind the wheel. He chose the latter.

As I sat there, taking in the pristine glass that protected the inside from the raw and gritty streets that New York City housed, I knew I had to get out from behind this wheel, hand my keys to the valet, and walk into the building that housed a broken heart—a heart that was once whole. The healed heart that I had the pleasure of holding, assuring, and protecting behind these walls. This building was more than just a building to me. The more I stared at the entrance, the more memories came flooding back to me. Memories of us arguing, making up, and then laughing at the foolish shit we argued about. This building had witnessed us both fall apart and then build each other back up. It held things neither of us dared to utter outside the walls of this building.

As I sat in the car, I watched an older white man come up the block and dap the young valet attendant. He was the doorman. I remember when he used to open the door for me late at night when I came in with my eyes so low because I would rather sleep when I was dead than let my woman take care of me. Every time I walked down that long block, his pale face greeted me as he held the door open, never making any awkward conversation. He was there to do his job, and his smile let me know he saw me, and there was a mutual respect.

An unspoken alliance.

I wondered if he remembered me. If he would remember the broke man who also happened to be broken. The man who didn't belong on this side of the city, on that block with a building that housed people who made someone's salary in a day. The same broke man who was with that rich woman, who never made him feel less than and allowed him to pay for every meal, even if it was his last. He knew I never belonged; however, he never made me feel like I didn't.

Back then, he saw the woman in love with the boy who was trying to find his footing. A boy trying to find his way as a man so he could provide—as he had always been told to do. I was trying... dying to become everything I knew I could be.

Everything I had been raised to be.

Honestly, that was the reason I decided to leave her. It wasn't an impulsive decision; it was something I had thought about for a while and knew had to be done. As much as I loved Tatiana, it also haunted me. Being in her world, knowing I didn't belong there. That I would always be hidden. Her secret.

Whenever I would become lost in the view from her balcony, I would sit and wonder what it must have felt like to have something like this...as a man. Not just a visitor passing through overnight, but someone who walked in the front door and made it mine. Holding the keys, being acknowledged by my last name by the staff. Never having to check in with the front desk before being allowed up to the floor where I lived.

It was funny because the longer I sat out here, the more I felt like that lost man from back then—the man, cosplaying as a boy, who had no idea what he wanted or the means to provide for the woman he loved. I had to remind myself that the man who sat behind the wheel of this Rolls-Royce wasn't the same man who used to walk three blocks from the subway. I had everything I used to think was out of my reach.

Well, almost everything.

I had the money, control, and power. Still, when it came to Tatiana, I felt like that boy, praying she still had space in her heart for me.

I shifted in my seat, then flashed my headlights to signal the valet that I was ready. The doorman had gone inside, probably to put his stuff up and start his shift.

"You ready, boss?" he asked, looking at me as I got out of the car.

His hand was already reaching for the keys, eager to take my car and whip it around the block. It was likely the only time his ass would get to sit on the soft leather and handle a car of that caliber.

Without saying a word, I reached into my pocket, peeled off a couple of hundreds, and stuffed the bills into his hand along with the key fob.

"A…are you sure?" the valet stammered from behind me, his reaction letting me know he had never received such a large tip before.

The doorman standing there, waiting for his shift replacement, held the door open for me—already aware of my reason for being there.

It was a little after two in the morning, and his eyes looked tired. I'm sure all he wanted was to clock out and dive into bed before having to wake up and return to work again the next day.

"Welcome back, Mr. Kane."

Walking through the door, I made my way past the front desk and to the gold-rimmed elevator. I caught my reflection before the doors opened. Dressed down in a pair of sweats, a T-shirt, and the latest designer sneakers, I was still the same Nazir, only now with extra commas in my bank account, investments under my belt, and my family never wanting for anything.

The elevator took me up to her floor—the same floor she used to share with one other condo. Now, she owned the entire floor, and the elevator opened into the foyer. As it passed each floor, my heart thumped harder and faster.

Despite the changes to her condo, the elevator remained the same. In the corner to the left, I remember pinning her there while sucking on her neck. I could still smell that cherry lip gloss and her cool minty breath. Her soft moans while I attacked her neck with kisses and flicks of my tongue. The feeling of her arms wrapped around my neck while I held her close. Lost in my thoughts, the elevator chimed to let me know I had arrived.

I stood in the middle of the elevator, taking up space while waiting for it to open. As soon as the door opened, I saw a security team member standing in the foyer. He was eating a beef jerky stick and nodded when he saw me.

"Heard somebody coming up. Nigga at the front desk don't ever call and let us know somebody's coming up," Kilo, one of my top guards, rambled.

The night shift that worked the front desk slacked when it came to announcing visitors. Even knowing who I was, he should have called to give a heads-up, but he never did.

"Nigga probably on his phone or some shit," I said as I passed him and entered the rest of the home.

Home.

Even though I always turned down her attempts to get me to move in with her, this place always felt like home. Not because of the expensive bamboo floors or the million-dollar view, but because she had always been here—either sitting on the couch with her textbooks or standing in the kitchen trying to figure out how to work the state-of-the-art stove. As soon as I stepped over the threshold, broken from the cold world, her warmth was right there waiting for me. The air always smelled like her—santal and vanilla. The scent clung to her body like a six-month-old clings to its mother. Her smell always lingered in the air or on my clothes, even after she was no longer in the same room. My body always reacted to her. My heart steadied, and I could finally breathe easily. The noise in my head quieted enough for me to hear her. I didn't need to be Naz when I was in the confines of these walls. To her, I was Nazir, and that was who I could be.

As I walked further into the condo, my guard gradually lowered, and I found myself looking at pictures of Tatiana, my daughter, and a man. The wedding and beach ceremony photos made it clear that the man was her husband. Nazira was smiling brightly while standing in the middle of them. Tatiana matched her smile as she looked down at our creation. In the second picture, she was looking off into the distance while holding her husband's hand. But there was something I noticed. In the midst of happiness, she had a lost look in her eyes, as if she was desperately trying to find what she needed to keep the smile on her face.

Stepping into the living room, which had been transformed from the small space with the brown suede couch, I recalled how we used to sit there for hours, taking in the view her condo offered. Her head on my shoulder, her legs thrown across me—peace filled my entire being whenever we shared those moments. Even after all the years that had passed, that same feeling was still there. It was different, even heavier. But it felt real, like the place remembered me, too.

It had gone through a transition, too—becoming larger than it used to be, breaking down walls, and adding more elements of luxury to it.

Like me.

No matter how long I had been gone, my peace had remained behind these walls, residing in the heart of this home. The couch that had always been a source of comfort was now gone, replaced with a soft cream sectional facing an even larger view. The lights were off, the room only being illuminated by the city's lights and a lit candle that was on the coffee table. I walked toward the floor-to-ceiling window, almost afraid to be in that space.

"Don't blow out my candle," the voice said.

Before turning around, I looked out at that view.

"Our flight is early tomorrow. You should be asleep," I replied.

When I turned around, I finally saw her curled up on a chaise lounge behind a plant. The enclave was designed to be hidden, perfectly tucked away from the rest of the living space, but the view was still visible from there.

"I don't sleep much."

"Why?"

She cut her eyes and scoffed. "As if I'm going to give you the million reasons why I don't sleep much."

Her tone was sharp, but I accepted it because I felt I deserved it. Tatiana was broken, and I was the fucker who broke her.

I watched as she twisted the edge of her silk robe between her fingers—a nervous habit that only I knew about. She used to hold eye contact like it was a weapon. Never backing down, always staring straight through your soul. That stare could make the most confident man question his own existence. Now her gaze bounced from the floor to the walls, everywhere but on me. She couldn't give me the eye contact I desperately craved. She couldn't give me what I wanted from her because I was causing her pain just by existing in the life she had created without me.

For all the words she wanted to scream, she stayed quiet. I could tell from her body language that she wanted to scream at me that I broke her and call me a pussy, a liar, and anything but a child of God.

But her heart wouldn't allow it.

Despite the pain I had caused, her heart remembered the good times—the better version of me before it was tainted by my actions. The version that made her laugh and hugged her when no one else knew she needed one. The one who could read her like her favorite novel without her having to say a word. The man who whispered our future into her ear before I kissed her head and left.

Tatiana wanted to hate me. Everything inside her was torn between what she needed to do and what she wanted to do. She hated herself because she couldn't give me the hate she so desperately wanted to give. It was something I had to carry with me—something I wanted to work so hard to change within her. I was here to pick up the pieces and rebuild the heart I had broken. I've always been told to clean up my messes, and I had made a mess of the woman sitting in front of me.

Tatiana didn't cry. She didn't shout or slam her fist against my chest while demanding answers. She sat still. Almost too still. Behind that reserved look was a woman trying to hold herself together while quietly unraveling at the seams.

"That's fair," I muttered, because that was the only words that made sense in this moment.

Tatiana snorted, low and bitterly, as she reached for her laptop like the conversation was already done.

"There isn't anything that's fair," she said flatly, finally standing.

Her wide hips filled out the silk robe, forming perfect parentheses. I didn't move. Instead, I remained in place, wishing she would just brush against me once. I'd settle for that. I watched as she retreated into the kitchen as if searching for something—possibly peace amidst the chrome appliances and white marble countertops.

She placed her laptop on the island, flipped the screen up, and clicked a few buttons before turning to the espresso machine as if it was routine. One foot pressed on top of the other as she fidgeted, her fingers trembling enough to make my heart ache.

I moved closer, close enough to smell the steam from the machine mixed with her perfume that clung to the silk of her robe.

Tatiana didn't take her eyes off the espresso machine. I didn't need her to.

I stood behind her, saying nothing. Just standing there with my hands extended on either side of her and resting on the counter. My heart calmed because she was near.

Her ass was pressed against me as she kept focused on her cup. The machine came to life, spitting out the espresso into the mug. The bitter concoction was a reminder that she still couldn't sleep.

I shouldn't have cared what she drank or when she drank it. But who was I kidding? Everything about this woman was my business—the curve of her back, the weight in her silence, and the way she bit down on her bottom lip whenever she was deep in thought.

Like now.

I wanted to be with her, love her, and heal the wounds I caused within her, but she wouldn't let me in. Her vulnerability came at a cost, and no matter how much I had or acquired, it would be far too expensive for me to buy.

"Can I hug you, Tata?" I asked, my cool breath, with hints of bourbon, caressing her earlobe.

She sucked in her breath and remained stiff as a wig from a beauty supply store. Her body froze, and she looked as though she couldn't gather her words. I could tell she wanted me to, but was scared. If she allowed me to touch her, it might do more than just comfort her. It could break her open and maybe leave her even more terrified than she was now.

Gently removing one of my hands from the counter that cornered her, she grabbed the cup from the machine and looked at me briefly. "Good night, Nazir."

I watched her gently close her laptop and leave the kitchen. I wanted to follow her but knew that wasn't fair. Everything was my fault, and it was selfish to try and force anything. She had to want me as much as I still wanted her.

I went back into the living room and sat on the couch, resting my head back as I took in the view—a view I had witnessed so many nights before. The only difference was that I used to have her lying with me when I took them in...and I planned to have it that way again one day.

"Mrs. Sterling, don't worry. We'll get everything with your jet squared away. As a courtesy, we're placing you on one of our company jets. Complimentary, of course," the man said, his words coming out as quickly as the sweat pouring from his forehead.

He stammered over every word while nervously tugging at the collar of his blazer like it would save him. He looked like someone who realized he had fucked up...or someone who was hiding some shit.

Tatiana remained poised. Her shoulders back, head slightly tilted. My baby never let shit rattle her, so she would be damned if she allowed anyone see her upset. Even with her eyes hiding behind those dark shades, I could still see that look she was giving him—one he should have been blessed he didn't have to see.

She didn't speak, and her lack of words continued to send this man into a spiral with more sweat pouring from his pores. Yaya stood to her left, her arms crossed, glancing between her best friend and the man who I thought would turn into a puddle at any second.

"Why wasn't I notified that there was an issue with the jet?" Tatiana asked, finally breaking her silence.

Her voice was even–calm with a hint of irritation laced within her words. The man blinked a few times like he thought it would be worse.

"We…we called, Mrs. Sterling. There must have been some miscommunication between the team. We've always been instructed to call." He paused as he quickly snatched the iPad from the assistant standing beside him. "Carlotta."

"I don't remember Carlotta telling me anything about the jet." Tatiana looked over at Yaya. "Did she say anything to you?"

Yaya raised both brows. "No. I would remember if she told me something like that. So, who exactly did *you* contact?"

For a second, he thought he had gotten her off his back. His face fell when he had both of them questioning him. His lips parted, but no sound came out. His silence irritated Yaya, who continued to give him looks until he finally parted those lips, and words fell out.

"We have the best team fixing the issue. In the meantime, do you want to rest in the lounge while the jet is being fueled?"

Tatiana exhaled through her nose. "Fix this shit."

Without waiting for him to make false promises and apologies, she turned around and went toward the lounge. Yaya remained as she pulled her phone out to start confirming his story.

I followed behind Tatiana as she stepped into the lounge, plopping into one of the armchairs like she had finally processed what he had told her. She wore a pair of wide-leg sweats, designer sneakers, and an oversized crop top that hung just right off her shoulder. The travel Chanel bag was stuffed to the brim with her laptop and any and everything she would need for the flight. It sat slouched in the seat beside her like it knew everything wasn't going as planned. We were supposed to be airborne, but now we were seated, waiting for them to tell us when the jet would be fueled.

I watched as she messed in her hair. It had been in a tight bun earlier when she iced homie back at the desk. Now, it was pulled loose, falling wild onto her shoulders as she ran her hand through it continuously. Frustration clouded the small space between us, and she didn't have to remove her dark shades for me to know.

I took the seat across from her. Even with her shades on, she wouldn't look at me. Not even a turn in my direction. I watched her.

Every breath, the shift of her fingers through her curls. Last night was etched in my brain. The memory of being that close to her.

Close enough to kiss her neck, smell her curls, and feel her ass pressed against me. Her voice was shaky, breathless as she tried to stand firm on her beliefs, her walls contemplating coming down. Just enough for me to taste what I had been missing for years.

I wanted to be closer.

I wanted to be buried inside of her again—not just in the physical sense, but deep enough to remind her who we were and who we could be. I wanted to spell my apology into her skin.

Stroke for stroke.

Until she stopped trying to hate me and just let herself feel again.

Every time I looked at her, flashes hit me. Tatiana under me, arching her back because she needed more. Her mouth open, eyes filled with love and lust while locked on mine. Begging me to go deeper, like she needed to forget every lie I ever told.

I needed that.

She did, too.

Letting out a deep breath, she looked at her watch again. "I have a few meetings today. We were supposed to be in the air, and now I'm stuck here waiting for them to fuel the jet."

Leaning forward, I looked at her. "What you want me to do, Tata?"

She finally turned to stare at me, never removing those glasses.

"What can you do? You can't make them fuel the jet quicker, and you damn sure can't get me up in the air in the next fifteen minutes."

I remained quiet and looked at her for a few minutes before I got up. She had received a call as I made my way back towards the front.

"How much longer?" I asked, staring directly at him.

I wanted my answer to come from him, not the bullshit assistant standing beside him. The man who had been sweating bullets five minutes ago was gone. He stood straight, his suit jacket buttoned, and his hair smoothed back like he wasn't sweating and apologizing moments before. That panic and nervousness he had in his eyes had vanished, and it had been replaced with a calm customer service tone. That tone that pissed you off when you were trying to get a payment arrangement, and they just told you no, then proceeded to apologize like that would keep your lights from being turned off.

He was back in control.

A few other clients had come in with their luggage as he held the phone to his ear. "At least another two hours."

"Same thing he just told me," Yaya responded, standing near the fancy-ass champagne vending machine.

"Enjoy anything from the lounge in the meantime." His tone was clipped, and he was dismissing us.

This wasn't the man who was tripping all over himself in front of Tatiana moments earlier. His tone told me that he thought I wasn't important, and I was just the help. In his eyes, he didn't think I should have been asking questions.

Better seen, never heard.

"He's a rude bitch who only acts one way in front of Tatiana because he's scared of both Raphael and her father. When it comes to anybody with her, he doesn't give a shit about them. We are all considered her help and shouldn't have anything to say. If anything, he thinks we should be grateful for the experience." Yaya confirmed exactly what I had been thinking.

"Oh yeah?"

"Hi, Mr. and Mrs. Cello. We will have you up in the air in fifteen minutes. We're doing a final cabin check on our jet to make sure everything is perfect for you."

The bald white man chuckled, that rich kind of chuckle. But I knew he wasn't that rich because he was chartering one of their jets instead of having his own stored there.

"We appreciate the very last-minute accommodation."

"Anything for our loyal clients. The lounge is right through there. Take a seat, and we'll come get your luggage when it's time."

They smiled as they both rolled their carry-on while leaving the three big pieces of luggage in the lobby.

"You have a jet ready right away for them but not Mrs. Sterling."

"Yes. We have multiple jets so we can accommodate our clientele. Who are you again? I never got your name."

He wasn't asking because he genuinely cared to address me correctly. The bitch was asking because he wanted to remind me of my position. It was his way of putting me in my place in a classy way.

As I approached the front desk, the phone rang, and he picked it up. The assistant looked at me, then quickly looked away. He knew how to read a room and didn't care to put his boss onto what was about to take place.

"The Hamptons this weekend? Ugh…maybe. I have to see what my schedule is looking like... Oh? He's going to be there? Well, I might have to." He faked a cough. "Pretend to be sick."

The person on the other end must have laughed, because he returned their laugh with an even faker one. I had very little patience, and mine had run with him. I pressed the receiver button, ending their call. He gasped and stared at me in shock.

"Look, I don't like doing all that yelling and shit that I know you're expecting from me. It's not even my flow on the real. That jet that's gonna be ready in fifteen minutes, make sure the name is switched to Tatiana Sterling and guests."

He snatched his hand back, appalled.

"That is against company policy, and I will do no such thing." He placed the phone back down on the receiver.

"Not even worth it. We can just wait," Yaya said from behind me as she stood a little distance away.

The smirk that curled at both ends of his lips pissed me off. He was waiting for me to accept defeat and go sit back down. Before he could react, I snatched his ass over the desk and grabbed the phone. Using the cord, I wrapped it around his neck while he screamed out.

Yaya quickly walked over toward the lounge and closed the doors, since people were coming out to see what all the commotion was about.

"I asked you nicely, and I'm not even all that nice. Gave yo' ass a chance to fix the fuck-up on your end. You will switch the paperwork and make sure the jet is properly fueled in ten minutes. Yo, Ya! Where they going?"

She walked to behind the desk and shuffled through the papers that he had laid out perfectly for their departure. "London."

I chuckled. "No need to worry. Las Vegas is a shorter distance than London. Have those papers switched, or I'm going to squeeze this bitch tighter every time that nigga over there blinks. Oh, shit...he blinked." I pulled the cord tighter around his neck.

"Ughhh..." he gargled, trying to catch his breath as his eyes bulged in his sockets.

"Stop playing games with me and get us the fuck out of here before I do some shit that you won't be able to catch your breath from."

I released him and swung his ass across the floor, the force propelling him until his back hit the champagne vending machine. Taking a breath, he held his neck while trying to regulate his breathing. I cracked my knuckles and looked at the assistant, who was already shuffling through papers with Yaya to get us out of here.

"We...we have all the paperwork and will...will have your bags put onto that jet," the assistant stammered, scared that his ass would be next.

"By the time my ass hits that seat in there, you better be coming to get us," I threatened and opened the doors.

Tatiana and the couple who had come in minutes before were staring at me, looking alarmed.

"What happened out there?" she asked.

She had finally taken off her glasses and was staring directly at me. My pretty baby was allowing me to look into her eyes, and that shit meant more to me than the shit I had just done.

"Something about the new wax they use on the floors. He's all good now. They got the emergency aid kit and all that shit," I said, sitting down in the seat across from her.

My bullshit explanation was enough for the couple, who went back to their conversation while Tatiana stared at me.

"What did you do?"

"You're stressed. So papa had to handle that shit for yo—"

"Mrs. Sterling, you are able to board the jet. Do…do you need anything specifically stocked onto the jet?"

That bitch came back with a red neck and a better attitude.

The shit was all his fault anyway. If he had come correctly, we wouldn't have had to have a conversation that involved violence. He's lucky I had self-control, because I really wanted to crack his fucking neck for the way he acted.

He stared at me for a moment before quickly rushing out of the lounge to get whatever Tatiana told him we needed.

Tatiana had a small smirk on her face as she looked at me. "Slippery floors, huh?"

"Damn floors."

I didn't need to tell her what I had done because she already knew, and I could tell she was thankful by the smile she allowed me to witness. All of this was on her time, and I would take the pieces she would give me. Even if she gave me crumb by crumb, I would accept each piece until I was able to form my own loaf of bread.

The mistake wasn't the delay. Shit, it wasn't even the switching of the jet. It was his ass thinking I was just some man—not knowing I would be *her* man.

CHAPTER THIRTEEN

Yaya

"Emotion" by Destiny's Child

DURING THE ENTIRE flight to Las Vegas, I watched Nazir as he watched Tatiana, who had been absorbed in her work. Her head was in her laptop the whole time. The only break she took was a quick power nap, as she called them. Every time she moved, made a sound, or just ran her hand through her curls, his eyes were fixed on her. Whenever we flew, she preferred to sit alone, not wanting anyone to crowd her space.

When we landed, we were whisked to the hotel, where they welcomed us like royalty. In a way, my best friend was some form of royalty. Both of her last names carried weight and demanded a different kind of respect that she often fought to have extended to me. Tatiana was constantly on the neck of anyone who didn't treat me the same as her, but when she wasn't looking, they still gave those looks that said I should've been grateful to be there.

They took Tatiana up the back elevator to her one-bedroom suite on the top floor of the hotel. I was handed my key card and shown to my upgraded room with a beautiful balcony that overlooked the famous water show.

After unpacking my clothes, I checked emails and tried to check in with Bloom. It was hard to get her on the phone these days. Every time I called, it went to voicemail, or she'd claim her phone had died.

She was distant now. It wasn't like she was cold and brushed me off; Bloom seemed like she was somewhere else. It was as if she had secrets she wouldn't open up and share with me. I remember the times when we used to tell each other everything.

With Sav locked up, I thought maybe things would shift in our relationship. I had hoped that the tension we felt when Sav was around would ease, and we could get everything back on track. I missed laughing with my sister and our late-night gas station runs, where we would sit in the car and talk about everything or nothing at all. Or when we would stay on the phone until sunrise and then fall asleep still on the line.

Tatiana was my best friend and I loved our bond, but there was something about the connection I had with my sister. It was hard when you felt like someone you loved was gradually slipping out of your grasp, and there wasn't anything you could do. I tried to give her space and not crowd her with my opinions or views, thinking it would help us grow closer. If anything, she pulled away even more.

I knew a lot of her distance had to do with Sav. She disliked her—to put it mildly—and thought I was settling. She said Sav made me small, and I just accepted it because I thought I was in love. I really did. I believed Sav was my forever, and I had finally found the person meant for me. Maybe Bloom was right, but I struggled to admit it—not just to her, but to myself, too.

My phone chimed, cutting through the silence I had found myself in. The screen lit up in the dark, casting a glow across the room where I had fallen asleep. I kept staring at the high vaulted ceiling, praying it was her. Maybe she saw my missed call and wanted to talk. My hand blindly felt around on the night table until I secured the phone within my hand. Bringing it toward my face, I looked at the text message.

Jonah: *Open the door.*

I stared at the screen for a few more seconds before pulling the covers from my body. The warm breeze floating through the curtains of the open balcony door explained why I slept so well.

Snatching my oversized college T-shirt off the table in the corner, I pulled it over my bare chest and panties while slowly walking toward the door.

Standing on my toes, I peered through the peephole, then quickly unlocked and opened the door to see Jonah standing there. He was dressed down in a grey sweatsuit, luggage in one hand, over-the-ear headphones hanging around his neck. His facial expression told me that he was pissed off. His jaw was clenched, like he was two seconds from making someone regret breathing the wrong way. I pulled the door open wider, letting him in, and slowly shut it behind us.

"What happened?"

He dropped his backpack onto the small table by the door with a thud, setting the headphones beside it.

"Makes sense why they wanted the meeting to be this weekend." Jonah muttered, his voice low and heated.

He peeled his hoodie from his body, tossing it over his suitcase. Everything about the way he moved around my room screamed that he wanted to rip someone's head off.

"Why?"

He was pacing again, muttering, too deep in his head to even realize he had ignored my question.

"I finally land after a long-ass flight, and you think a driver would be waiting, right?" He scoffed, getting upset all over again. "Nah. No driver. I shook the shit off and caught an Uber to the hotel, ready to shower and get some sleep before tomorr—"

"You flew commercial?" I interrupted without thinking.

Jonah turned and looked at me like I had just spit in his face.

"The fuck is wrong with commercial, Yalina?" he snapped, eyes narrowing. "You think I'm about to waste jet fuel for one damn person?"

I held my hands up, smirking a little. "I was just asking a question. Damn."

Jonah shook his head, muttering something under his breath about being spoiled, as he dropped onto the edge of the bed, rubbing the back of his neck like the day had beat the shit out of him.

"That big-ass wellness spa conference is this weekend. My room was overbooked, apparently, and the bitch at the desk said I needed to wait until morning for a manager."

It made sense why it was so packed when we were checking in earlier.

"I should call and wake that bitch up right now. What they mean overbooked? He asked us to come here." He continued to massage his neck while muttering to himself.

Jonah wasn't the type who said things just to say them. If he said it, he meant every word. I had about four seconds to talk to him down before he made it everybody's problem.

"You don't need to blow it up right now." I quickly jumped in. "My room's got enough space. You can crash here for the night."

He lifted his head and locked eyes with me. "Why the fuck you think I'm here, Yummy? I was staying with you anyway."

I rolled my eyes and crossed the room to grab my phone from the nightstand. The screen lit up. It was a little after midnight, and I didn't have the energy to argue with him about how he was in the process of hijacking my room.

"Guess you can sleep over there on the couch," I said flatly, nodding toward the velvet kidney bean-shaped couch in the corner.

He chuckled low, like I was a joke to him or something.

"I'm not sleeping on that uncomfortable shit," he said, stretching like he was already claiming my bed. "We both know those couches are for decoration. I'm in the bed with you tonight."

It was how his low eyes roamed from my face to my body.

His voice dropped. "How does that make you feel, Yalina?"

It was always the way he said it.

My real name.

He said it with such passion that I often found myself second-guessing what I heard. Maybe I was envisioning something that wasn't happening. It always made me feel a surge of heat in my chest. Unexpected, and always impossible to ignore. It was like he lifted my shirt and dropped coal straight down the front. He was peeling back a layer I hadn't let anyone touch in years.

I didn't respond right away.

I couldn't.

Because if I opened my mouth, he would hear the tone, the passion, the silent moans behind the words. Granting him the permission he knew he never needed to ask, because it had been silently given.

Breaking out of the trance he unknowingly put me in, I went into the mini fridge and grabbed two bottles of overpriced water.

"Whatever, Jonah. Stay on your side, and I will stay on mine," I said, setting the boundaries and tossing one bottle to him.

He caught it with one hand, cracked it open, and took a gulp. The room became quiet while he finished the water. It wasn't an awkward silence…just tense.

I felt the shift. I'm pretty sure he felt it, too. But neither of us wanted to say anything. I would rather pretend I didn't feel the shift in hopes that he would do the same.

I busied myself with some of the clothes I had left on the couch before my nap. I folded and refolded the clothes I knew I would wear the next day. With my back turned toward him, I could still tell he was sitting with his elbow on his knees and the empty water bottle dangling from his fingers. When I finally turned around, he was already looking right at me as if he had been watching my back the whole time. I pretended to fold the clothes that were already folded. His stare wasn't like his usual stare.

He was staring through me like he was seeing me for the first time.

Really seeing me.

Seeing the Yalina not everyone got to experience. It was the me that I kept locked away, never allowing someone to experience me in this way. Since being with Sav, I had hidden this Yalina. It didn't make sense for her to experience this side of me when that wasn't who she wanted.

"You ain't gotta keep moving around like you busy, Yummy." His voice was low, slightly rough with an edge of sleepiness in it. "You tired…come get in the bed."

He wasn't suggesting it. He was telling me.

The nervousness spread through my body like a chill on a windy day. My stomach spoke before I could, and I was thankful only I heard it. Getting into that bed meant I would have to unpack some things, and this wasn't the right moment or the right time. Not when it was after midnight, and the only thing between us was a small decorative pillow.

I sat my folded shirt down on the couch and crossed the room, sinking down onto the other side of the bed without looking his way. He remained at the end of the bed before he stood up. He was standing there like he knew he looked good. Who was I kidding? Jonah was fine.

That little grin could get anything out of any woman, including me. Unlike the hoes he messed with, I had restraint and would never allow his charming smile, beautiful face, and sexy body to convert me to the dark side.

Jonah was the dark side.

He took his shirt off, exposing his caramel skin—every inch of it covered in detailed tattoos that had a purpose and a story. I felt like I could read his entire life story across his body if I looked long enough.

And only God knew that I was looking.

His abs were sculpted, his arms thick enough to carry all that arrogance he possessed. And his beard? *Jesus.* Jonah's beard had no business being that full, that clean. As if he went to angels to get his lineup. He always wore two gold chains that rested on his chest, and I imagined them swinging in my face as he hovered over me.

Yalina, stop.

With his shirt off, my attention was now drawn to his sweatpants, which sat low on his waist. Was he doing this on purpose? Was it both a warning and an invitation? His eyes had always been the problem for me. Quiet and intense, like he could see through me. It was like he wanted to say something slick and was waiting for me to slip. Maybe I did want to see what he would do with me. Still, I played it cool like always.

When he turned around, those lips curled into that grin. His lips were the kind that made you pause mid-argument, because even when he was tight-lipped, they looked good enough to suck on. And the Lord knew I wanted to suck on them. His nose was strong, straight, and fitting. Jonah might have come off like a pretty boy, but he had that grown man face—like he'd been through some shit and even participated in it. He wasn't the kind of man who went down easy.

It didn't matter how fine he was, though. It was dangerous for me to feel this way about him. I wasn't going to be that girl who falls for a man while being in a relationship.

I couldn't be her.

When he went to take a shower, I quickly grabbed my phone and called Tatiana. She was the only person I could talk to about this. She answered the phone sounding wide awake. If there ever came a day when she picked up the phone and sounded half asleep, I would be shocked as hell. Sleep and my girl didn't mix, and I hated that for her.

"I'm assuming you took the best nap once you were settled."

I snickered. "The best nap—mouth all wide open and drool on the pillow."

She laughed. "Good. You need the sleep. You're always so busy working."

"I could say the same about you. Why are you even up right now? And don't blame it on the time change either."

"In my defense, there's a beautiful terrace attached to my suite, and I did take a nap on the lounge out there."

"I won't complain or get on your case since you took a slight nap. But knowing you, it was only a fifteen-minute nap."

"Ten minutes, because Rick Valora came to my suite to have a quick chat over tea. You know rich people."

I snorted. "You are rich people, Tatiana."

"Not that type, I suppose. Anyway, why are you calling me?"

I pulled my legs up to my chest and started rubbing the scar from my childhood. I was seven years old, and my cousin was teaching me how to ride a bike. I fell in the process, scraping my knees and crying at the sight of the blood. But no sooner than my mother cleaned up my cuts, I was right back out there on that bike, determined to master riding it in one summer afternoon. The scar was still visible and a reminder of my tenacity.

"Jonah's room was overbooked, so he's staying in mine."

"Hmm."

"What's that sound?"

"You on birth control, right?"

I laughed. "Tatiana."

"What? I'm asking because the sexual tension between you two is thicker than me. Does your room have a pull-out couch?"

"No."

"Yeah, be ready to toot that ass up, Yaya. Or should I call you Yummy?"

I climbed out of the bed and walked onto the balcony. The water show was now dark, but the lights of Las Vegas were still brighter than ever.

"I'm not going to sleep with him. I mean, the thought is there, but we can't do that. We share a godchild together, and it would only complicate things."

"If that's the excuse you want to use, I'm going to let you have that," she replied, chewing in my ear.

"I have a girlfriend, remember? I'm not that kind of girl who just does someone wrong," I replied, even though my mind was telling me that my relationship with Sav was over. I just needed my heart to agree.

The line went quiet. I knew what Tatiana wanted to say without her actually saying it. She finally broke the silence, her voice low and steady. She was coming from a place of love, and I knew that before the words even left her mouth.

"You were never really happy with Sav, Yaya. Not once."

I remained quiet, allowing her to continue.

"How many times did you cry over that girl? How many times have I stayed up on the phone with you while you waited for her to come home at night? Yaya, you begged her to leave the streets alone—handed her chances most people would give their life for—and she spat in your face every time."

I closed my eyes, swallowing the lump that formed. It hit me hard because every word she said was the truth. She had front row seats to witnessing the shit I put up with Sav—all the broken promises, disrespect, and arguments. Tatiana was always there to listen while I vented.

She cleared her throat, still not done expressing how she felt. "Sav could dish out judgment to everybody else like she was the second coming, but when it came to listening? To growing with you and having the life you told her you wanted, she could never choose you, babe. Never."

Her voice cracked slightly. It wasn't because she was upset with me, but because she hated to see me hurt. See me clinging to a dead branch that offered me nothing. The leaves were gone, and the branch was falling apart right in my hands, but I kept trying to water it, hoping to revive what was already dead. If I were honest with myself, there was nothing left to do but put that branch down and move on with my life.

"I hear you, Tati."

"You keep loving her despite receiving nothing but scraps in return, Yaya. She never poured into you the way you have poured into her, loved her, and chose her."

The heavy silence on the line filled me with emotion. I quickly wiped away the tears that were slowly rolling down my cheeks. What could I say? She was right.

Tatiana had sat back and allowed me to live my life while always showing up when I needed her. Now, she was speaking the truth, letting me know this wasn't healthy, and I couldn't keep going on like this with Sav.

I finally cleared my throat, forcing out the words despite how heavy they felt.

"She's just… Tati, she's been through a lot. It's not easy for her to trust people or change."

My voice wasn't even convincing to myself, so I knew Tatiana could see right through what I had said to her. The silence on the other end of the line confirmed what I already knew.

She released a sigh, not one that was rude; she was just tired. Tired of me having the strength to defend someone who wouldn't defend me.

"You make excuses for her. Cover for her, love her, fight for her. Name a time when she has done those things for you?"

I tried to respond, even defend myself, but I couldn't. The words wouldn't form, and my mouth became dry as cotton while trying to find the right words.

Her voice softened. "Do you ever think that maybe you're trying to heal a version of her that never existed in the first place?

"Can we talk tomorrow?" I said, attempting to abruptly end the call.

By this point, the tears were streaming down my face because I had gotten exactly what I called her for—a dose of reality that I needed. A reminder that I had to stop living in some fantasy world that didn't exist.

"I love you, Yaya. Get some sleep. We can talk about it tomorrow, or even better, we can get together for a girls' night round table with lots of wine."

I laughed through the tears while wiping them away. "This conversation, coupled with wine, sounds like the best idea."

"Get some sleep."

"You, too."

"Eh, just get enough for both of us," she said before hanging up.

Deep down, I always knew the truth. I wasn't in love with the woman Sav was; I loved the woman I hoped to shape her into. She was my passion project, the acknowledgment I sought to prove she could change. I had written this love story of what our relationship could be with a version of her that never existed and never could.

After sitting on the balcony for a few, I wiped my eyes one last time and went inside, closing the door behind me. I rummaged through my purse for my favorite makeup wipes and used them to clean my face of the tears. Climbing into bed, I checked my phone for any notifications from my sister before turning on the TV, but I wasn't really paying attention to what was on the screen.

The bathroom door cracked open, steam following behind Jonah like he had sparked up in there. He had his towel wrapped around his waist, another in his hand, as he draped it around his neck. His skin shimmered, his tattoos glistening, and his beard dripped with beads of water. I quickly tried to act normal while still staring at an infomercial that I hadn't even noticed I had been watching.

Normal.

What did that even mean? I was trying to act normal, like I hadn't just been on the phone getting some real-life advice that I still wasn't sure I was in the place to receive. Jonah wasn't dumb, and from the way he paused in front of the TV and stared directly at me, I could tell he knew I had been crying.

He pulled the towel from around his neck and dried his beard, never breaking our eye contact. One stupid tear fell down my face, and that was when the concerned entered his eyes.

He cared.

"What's wrong, Yummy?" he asked, his voice low.

It wasn't his typical tone. There wasn't a hint of humor or teasing behind his question. His tone was softer, concerned, desperate to know what the problem was so he could fix it. I shook my head quickly, praying that if I moved quick enough, that one tear wouldn't have any company.

"Nothing. Stupid show has me crying," I lied and grabbed my phone so it could distract me.

If Bloom loved me, she would call right this second and give me a reason to avoid this conversation, I thought to myself. *It's one thing to have this type of conversation with my best friend, but I certainly don't want to have it with Jonah.*

"Yalina," he said, speaking even softer this time.

He stepped closer, slow and deliberate, studying me as if he could see the cracks in my foundation. I couldn't look up at him because the dam would break, and I would look foolish. Jonah never got to see this side of me. He saw the woman who helped Tatiana run her entire life—the woman who was quick on her feet and a hard worker, determined to prove to her best friend that she was grateful for all the opportunities she had given her.

"I promise I'm alright, Jonah," I lied.

He towered over me, and I refused to look up because I knew I'd have to lie to him, and I wasn't sure if I wanted to. I felt a dip in the bed as I kept staring at my phone, pretending I was doing anything to avoid having to look into his eyes. The lump in my throat continued to grow, and I nearly choked myself trying to push it back down.

Jonah didn't say anything or try to force anything out of me. Instead, he remained seated on my side of the bed, still wrapped in his towel. The heat continued to rise from his skin, as if he had used all of the hot water the hotel offered while showering. He was close enough that I could feel him. So close that if I leaned slightly, I would fall right into him.

For a while neither of us said anything. We just remained quiet, only soft breaths being heard between the both of us. Jonah held space for me to come to him if I wanted to. I hated how much I wanted to be in his space and how much my hands trembled as I set my phone on the nightstand.

His eyes roamed to my hand, watching as I placed my phone down. Then he slowly reached for me and gently pulled me closer to him. His hand graced the side of my thigh as he stared in my eyes. He was asking me a silent question, and I had granted him silent permission. No words were needed because we both could read each other's mind in this moment. His eyes were low with temptation as he held me.

I don't know if I was overly tired, or Tatiana's voice was echoing in my ears, or just the way this man saw me. He truly saw me when I didn't want to be seen. It was a gift not many people had, but he did.

Leaning into him, I pressed my forehead into his shoulder and broke down sobbing. He wrapped his arms around me without hesitation. He didn't need to ask any questions or try to fix the problem right then. He only wanted to comfort me.

His big, steady arm wrapped around my body, pulling me into his warmth. Jonah was patient, not rushing me. He was just here, allowing me to get everything out without asking a million questions. His hand slid up my back, rubbing it slowly, the way you would calm somebody who didn't know how to fall apart properly.

"You don't always have to be the strong one, mama," he mumbled into my shoulder, his voice low and rough against my skin. "Never with me."

Though his words were meant to comfort me, they caused me to break down even more. Because for the first time in a long time, I believed it.

CHAPTER FOURTEEN

Tatiana

MY BREATH CAUGHT in my chest when I closed my eyes, visualizing Nazir standing behind me in the kitchen a few days ago. I wanted to spin around, press my lips to his, and let his hands explore my entire body. Nazir always knew my spots without me ever needing to tell him. One look from me, and he was ready to flip me over and make me scream his name.

Stroke his ego.

Because he knew exactly what he was doing when it came to his way around a woman's body—my body.

I straightened myself up in the meeting and continued to listen to every reason we should consider adding a Hush location in The Valora. Ricky Valora was pulling out all the stops, especially since Jonah had given him an earful this morning about his room being overbooked. To make up for it, he offered his apologies and put both Yaya and Jonah in a two-bedroom suite with the same view I had in my suite.

He wanted Hush in his hotel more than he wanted to wear that tacky gold watch he sported on his tanned wrist. My facial expression stayed neutral, never giving him too much. I smiled at the presentation and the numbers he projected we would make. The money was great, but I had learned that all money wasn't good money. The money wouldn't be worth shit if the partnership wasn't shit.

I watched Jonah sitting with dark sunglasses on, Yaya beside him. There was something different between the two of them. They hadn't had sex, because I would have been able to sniff that out a mile away. It was something different that I couldn't put my finger on.

Yaya glanced over at me briefly before she went back to taking notes and listening to whatever Ricky was talking about.

We were supposed to fly in the day before, have the meeting the next day, and then decide whether to move forward before flying back home that same day. Instead, we were going to end up staying a full weekend due to the wellness conference. Every spa attended this conference annually, which made it funny that The Valora was hosting the conference this year.

"If everything checks out on your end, I think it would be a good idea for us to make the announcement this weekend," Ricky suggested.

"Why the fuck would we make the announcement this weekend? That would be jumping the gun, no?"

Ricky sat down and looked at Jonah. "This would be a great move for both of us. Our hotel is the only six-star hotel in Las Vegas. Adding Hush to our location would only further build the small brand's name."

A hand pushed a chilled glass of water in front of me, and I looked up. My eyes locked with Nazir, as his facial expression remained stoic.

"Thanks."

He nodded and returned to the door where he had been standing for most of this meeting. I took a sip of the water and watched as Ricky and Jonah went back and forth.

"Small brand?" Yaya snorted, like she had just processed what he had said.

"You have one location, am I right?"

"Yes," I replied, then allowed him to further flesh out what the fuck he meant by referring to my spa as a "small" brand.

He sat back and fixed his suit jacket before continuing.

"We have some well-known spas with locations nationwide interested in partnering with us. The Valora started as a boutique hotel, and look at what we've achieved. That's why I want this to work between us."

"That's where you're wrong, Ricky. I don't want Hush to expand across the country. My spa does numbers as if it has a location in every state and internationally. It's based in a small town just an hour from New York City, yet we attract clients from near and far."

"Somebody didn't take the time to read over our mission statement," Yaya muttered as Ricky turned red from being embarrassed.

Hush was a passion project, something I needed to do while navigating uncertainty and rediscovering myself *outside* of motherhood. We knew every client who walked through our doors and witnessed them come in broken down and leave refreshed. During the holidays, I would rent out Miller's Pointe for a Christmas party and give yearly bonuses to my staff because they deserved it for all of their hard work. I didn't need anyone to tell me anything because my business was small enough for me to know.

My fear was that if I decided to scale bigger, I would lose that small-town feeling. I knew it was necessary because our waitlist was fully booked for at least a year, as people were eager to experience what we offered. But the thought of expanding still scared me.

The meeting in the Dominican Republic was the only one I was excited about. Two locations in the US and one in the Caribbean were all we needed. I agreed to this meeting already knowing that I wouldn't be impressed and that I wouldn't want to move forward with a partnership.

I couldn't let him know that, though.

My father had always told me to treat business like poker. Never let them know your next move until you know that it's a win.

"We heard what you can offer us if we choose to put our location in your hotel. I think we all have a lot to discuss and see the actual numbers, and then we'll be in touch." I stood up, ready to get out of my heels and actually enjoy some food.

I spent the day between different meetings and even allowed Ricky to talk me into sitting through one of the conference panels. The panel was a reminder of why Hush had never attended this conference, and why I would continue to run my business the way I wanted. All the spas were so focused on copying each other. When I saw how interested Ricky was in the panel, I knew we wouldn't be the perfect mix. He would run Hush like all the other spas at the conference, and he would do it because he wanted to cater and please his hotel guests, not because he genuinely cared about the clients.

"Sounds like a plan. Do you need me to make a reservation for you at Alora? I heard it's like pulling teeth to eat there," he snickered, knowing he owned one of the most popular restaurants on the strip.

"We're good. I was able to get Mrs. Sterling a reservation," Nazir's baritone voice boomed across the conference room.

Ricky smiled nervously and shook Jonah's hand. "Perfect. Let me know if there is anything that you need from me while you're here in Vegas. Make sure to continue checking out the panels, too…some informative things."

"Some informative bullshit," Jonah mumbled.

Yaya tugged on his pant leg while looking up at him, and he looked down at her with a different expression. I wanted to know what happened in that room between them.

I needed to know.

Nazir held the door open for me, and I climbed into the back of the truck. Yaya and Jonah decided they would grab dinner together and then do some shopping. I wanted to change out of these clothes and get some food.

I popped a piece of gum into my mouth while looking over at him. "Don't tell me that you lied about the reservation."

He looked up from his phone. "Nah."

I watched as the driver took us back to the hotel, since the meeting was at a different hotel. Ricky's family owned a bunch of hotel chains in Las Vegas, but The Valora was their most well-known establishment.

Nazir's phone started ringing, and I busied myself out the window while pretending not to listen to his conversation.

"Yeah, I'm out here until Monday. I can come pick her up from my mom's house… Nat, you need to stop trying to handle everything. What did I tell you about that? I'm always going to be here, and I'm gonna handle it for you."

I couldn't hear what the woman was saying, but I knew he was speaking to a woman. My heart twisted when he told her he'd always handle things for her and be there for her. Where was that energy when I needed him?

"Got you. Have her call me when she's done playing with her friends." I could hear screaming coming from his phone as he laughed. "Alright, put her on."

My ears perked up. From his tone in how he said it, I could tell he had children—at least one. He couldn't convince me otherwise, and I would never believe it either.

"I'm working… I'll talk to her tonight… Bet."

He ended the call, but I refused to turn my face from staring out the window. I wouldn't let him see that I was bothered—hurt even. He couldn't see that my eyes were becoming misty because he was giving another little girl the father she deserved, while I had to lie to my daughter. Her life was an entire lie, and she would never forgive me once she understood what I had lied to her about.

As soon as the driver opened the door, I swung my purse onto my arm and headed inside the hotel. The doors seemed to open as if I were a genie, making them slide open with just a blink of the eye. Nazir followed behind me, making sure everyone knew he was my security. Before I could even scan the keycard to head up to the suite, his hand extended and scanned the card for the elevator.

The ride up to the suite was quiet, and I welcomed the silence. It was better than trying to figure out what to say or do, especially since he didn't owe me an explanation. I wanted to make that clear to him. What we had was in the past, and we could forget it ever happened. He could pretend Nazira didn't exist and continue on with his life.

Once we made it inside, I went straight to my room to shower and change for dinner.

Alora was a very expensive and fancy restaurant, and there were always celebrities dining there. Reservations were hard to get, which made me wonder how Nazir managed to get one. I knew I couldn't dress down in my favorite sweats and oversized hoodies.

Imagine someone snapping a picture of a celebrity, and I'm in the back, stuffing my face with a messy bun.

I quickly showered and rubbed on my favorite combination of santal oil and Jo Malone Beach Blossom. While I allowed my scent to settle before applying more oil and perfume, I curled my hair and put it in pin curls before doing my makeup.

A FaceTime call came through. It was my baby's name. I slid my finger across the screen to answer while I tended to applying my makeup.

"Hey, baby."

"Hi, Mom. What are you doing? I can't see you."

Her face was fully in the camera while I was doing my least favorite part of makeup— my eyeliner.

Guiding that pen across the rim of your eyelid was absolute torture; however, I had been doing it since high school, so I didn't think I could stop. My makeup felt incomplete without this step.

"Doing makeup, Zira."

"Man, I can't wait until I'm able to wear makeup."

She sulked, and I laughed because this had been a conversation in our home since she was five. Nazira always watched me do my makeup whenever she was home, and I loved seeing her expressions as I painted my face like I was performing magic right before her eyes. In a way, I was. These dark circles and marks weren't going to hide themselves, and I didn't get enough sleep to go into meetings without concealer.

"I don't know why you want to wear makeup when your skin is already amazing," I replied, finishing my makeup and propping up my phone.

"You look beautiful, Mom."

"Thanks, baby." I blushed at my daughter's compliment.

Nazira was someone who made me feel good. Anytime she saw me dressed up, she made it a point to compliment me. I always made sure to tell her how beautiful she was, and I think that's where she got it from.

"Where's Nazir?"

I looked at the phone, but she was looking at something on the counter, so she didn't see my alarmed facial expression.

"I'm sure he's around here somewhere...protecting the space."

"Oh, okay. I like that he has the same name as me."

I smiled. "Yeah, that is pretty cool. Aja hasn't come to pick you up yet?"

Nazira popped a grape into her mouth and shook her head no. "She's on her way."

"Is everything all packed and ready?"

"Yes, Mommy. I can't wait to swim in the pool and hang out with everyone," she said, excited to be around girls her age.

Aja's great niece was around her age, so I couldn't wait for her to come home and tell me all about it.

"You look beautiful. Where are you headed?" Bloom took the phone as Nazira hurried off to grab something she forgot.

Bloom propped the phone up on the counter and looked at me.

"Dinner with Nazir...I think. He said he made reservations but didn't say if he would be joining me."

"Hmm, dinner. That's a step in the right direction," she teased, knowing I would roll my eyes and wave her off.

"It's not even like that. Even if he does join me, do you expect me to forget everything for the sake of a meal?"

"Never said that. All I'm saying is you need to get out how you feel so that man can fuck you all up and through that hotel."

Bloom quickly covered her mouth and glanced around. Once she made sure Nazira was nowhere in earshot, she chuckled.

"I am not having sex with that man."

"Your man."

"Girl, bye."

Bloom chuckled and then sighed. "As much as you want to believe that the feelings aren't there, they are. The minute you saw him, those feelings came back."

"It really sounds like you want me to ignore the past and just jump his bones, Bloom." I brushed out my curls, made a side part, and sprayed some mist to keep the flyaways down.

"If you are so over him and this is water under the bridge, why are you so angry?"

I blankly stared at her through the screen. "I can be angry and *not* have feelings. Maybe you should try it."

"Pass me those chips, Emmy!" she hollered, and I saw her grab a bag of chips from someone out of the camera's view. "Girl, I don't catch feelings. Feelings end with you angry and hurt. I don't aspire to be either."

Since ending things with her boyfriend, who worked at the club, Bloom had no attachment to men or relationships. She was perfectly fine messing around, as long as there were no strings attached. I used to chalk it up to her free-spirited vibe and her not wanting any children.

Bloom was the eccentric, rich auntie who let the kids do whatever they wanted. At times, I couldn't tell who was watching who when she was with Nazira.

"Anyway, kiss my baby for me."

"Pop-Pop, what are you doing here?" I heard Nazira say in the background.

Bloom looked over her shoulder.

"My godfather is there?" I asked.

"Apparently so. I think Aja is in the car. Want to talk to him?"

I fixed my stubborn eyebrow. "No. I had emailed him yesterday. We have lunch plans when I'm back home. Kiss my baby for me and tell her that I love her."

"Will do."

I didn't need to ask what she was going to get into. Whenever she didn't have to watch Nazira, she usually went ghost for a few days and reappeared with the craziest stories.

My stomach growled loud enough for me to put some pep in my step. I quickly slipped into the golden silk dress waiting on the chair for me. The fabric caressed my body as it slid down, hugging every curve and draping perfectly. Golden against my skin, it highlighted every warm undertone, making me look like I'd been dipped in the sun. I looked like a thick Emmy award, and I couldn't be mad about it.

To break up all the gold, I applied a bold red lipstick, the color popping against my skin. Before giving myself a quick lookover, I grabbed my red Brandon Blackwood clutch, the perfect little accessory to tie it all together.

Staring at myself in the mirror one last time, I smoothed my hands down my hips and left the bedroom for the main living area. When I entered the kitchen, I saw roses on the counter with a card. I looked around, waiting for him to coolly make his appearance. Fumbling with the envelope, I read the note.

I don't need to see you to know you look beautiful. Come downstairs, dinner awaits…

Nazir.

I sniffed the roses before heading to the door, where security held it open for me. If Nazir couldn't be with me, he was going to make sure someone else was there to protect me. I took the elevator down to the lobby, and my heart fluttered. Why the hell was I so nervous? I shouldn't have been nervous because this wasn't a date. For all I knew, he had a table reserved just for me.

The elevator opened, and I stepped out into the nearly empty lobby. Across the lobby, I spotted him sitting by the water fountain. I would say we spotted each other at the same time, but

I was almost certain he saw me the moment I stepped out of the elevator.

I tried to walk to him, but he waved his finger no, leaving me to wait in the middle of the lobby. The minute he stood up, I took in his entire appearance. He was dressed in all black, wearing a short-sleeve fitted button-down shirt and matching black pants. On his feet, he had on a pair of designer sneakers.

His scent greeted me before he did, and I stood there trying to play it cool, pretending I never loved this man once upon a time. Who was I kidding? Had I ever stopped loving him? Maybe there was some truth in what Bloom had said. Maybe the reason I was so angry was because the feelings never truly left. They had been buried deep and only surfaced when he came near. When he finally approached me, he bit down on the corner of his lips as he examined me.

Staring down at me, he had a perfect view of everything I was wearing. If I had a closure, he would have seen that, too. The minute I raised my eyebrow was the moment he realized I was looking up at him, and he broke from his trance.

"You ready?" I asked.

"Shit, I don't fucking know now."

I looked confused. "What do you mean?"

"Tata…that dress on you. We can do room service," he suggested.

I waved him away and took a few steps forward, the echoes from my heels sounding throughout the lobby.

"I'm going to have a good dinner—either alone or with company. The choice is yours," I said, then turned and walked away.

The restaurant was within walking distance of the hotel, and the heels I wore were comfortable for a short walk. Like my own personal shadow, I felt Nazir come beside me.

"You look beautiful, Tata."

I smiled. "Thanks."

I could tell from the way he spoke—his voice rougher than it usually was—and the way his eyes roamed every inch of me that he wanted to say more.

Even do more.

Once we reached the restaurant, Nazir held the door open for me, his hand hovering at the small of my back as I walked in. His touch was innocent, simple even, and it nearly had me come undone. Feeling his hand on any part of my body caused it to become warm. Nazir knew the power he held over me, and years later, that power was still relevant.

The restaurant was dim, with small lamps provided so the patrons could see the menu. It whispered opulence, expensive, and every other word that meant *money*. Soft music floated through the air—that old school R&B. The kind you didn't realize you knew until you found yourself humming the song word for word.

The hostess led us to a private booth tucked away in the corner. As we settled into the velvet and gold accents, the hostess fucked Nazir with her eyes. His broad shoulders, height, tattoos, and brown skin glowing under the chandeliers made him enticing to her, and she couldn't pretend she wasn't attracted to him. He didn't care. Honestly, I don't think he noticed because his eyes had been locked on me since we walked into the restaurant. He probably only said two words to her, besides giving his name for the reservation.

Nazir slid into the booth across from me, stretching his arm along the backrest as if he owned the whole restaurant.

Comfortable.

Confident.

Far from the man who used to order water and let me get whatever I wanted. His aura had always been the same, and his confidence was always there. The money never was, and that's where his insecurity came in.

The silence surrounded us, and I found myself humming the words to an old-school song. I busied myself with the menu, pretending to read like I didn't notice his gaze burning a hole in the back of it. I knew the minute I put the menu down, his eyes would be ready to pierce beyond my soul.

When the waitress came, he ordered for both of us without asking me what I wanted. There was no need to ask or complain about him ordering my food. It was something he did. He knew me so well that he always ordered my favorite foods, and I never complained. This time, I was slightly nervous because just like things had changed for him over the years, they had changed for me, as well.

I hated how impressed and excited I was just from something as simple as ordering my food. The lump crawled up my throat just from him paying attention and doing what he had always done. The problem wasn't what he had always done, but what he had done. He never ran, and that was exactly what he did when it came to us.

When she set our drinks down, he finally spoke. "You look good, Tata."

That name.

It felt like heaven opened, and the angels were singing to me. I guess, in a way, it had always felt like that to me. It always felt like heaven because Nazir was that to me. I worshipped him like a god.

A leader.

And he let me down.

I quickly took a sip of my lychee martini and gathered the courage to look across the table into his eyes.

"It's just dinner. You don't need to compliment me all night like we're on a date."

My eyes scanned the restaurant, desperate to see anything but his gaze.

"Don't do that."

I sipped my drink again. "Do what?"

He picked up his bourbon slowly, lifting the glass to his thick lips and taking a sip, never wincing because we both knew bourbon puts hair on your chest—especially the specified-aged bourbon he requested.

"Pretend that this doesn't mean something to you."

Pressing my lips together and setting my glass back down, I fixed the end of the table curtain, desperate for anything to distract me.

"I don't have to pretend, Nazir. This is a dinner…a business dinner with my security."

"Damn."

The words hit harder than I wanted them to. Before I could try to fix things, the food arrived at the table. The heat from the plates created a barrier between us while the chef sliced and salted the Kobe A5 Wagyu ribeye in front of us.

Before he left, he thanked us for dining at the restaurant tonight and explained the way he cooked the steak. Apparently, whenever someone ordered this particular cut of beef, the chef would come out to properly slice and salt it for you. Everything was family-style, so we shared the side dishes. Nothing was to be touched by us because once the chef excused himself, two other staff member came to properly plate our food.

As they served us, Nazir leaned back with his arm still draped around the booth, and his drink in his other hand. He nodded to signal what he did or did not want.

When they were gone, I bowed my head to say grace and then cut into the steak. I've had my fair share of Wagyu, but the way this one was cooked should have been illegal. It was butter-soft and melted in my mouth as I chewed.

"So, have you ever been here before?"

He finally leaned forward, shrugging his shoulder. "A few times. Nothing like this, though."

I continued to busy myself with my food. "Like what? This restaurant? It's certainly an experience."

"I've been here before."

My eyes finally found their way to his.

"Like sitting across from you…someone I lost. In this seat, staring at how beautiful you look tonight, it's even more confirmation that I still want us more than I want to breathe, Tata."

That damn lump reappeared, and my vision slightly blurred. Not because of tears, but because this was something I had envisioned for years. What would a dinner with Nazir Kane look like?

It was easier to pretend I didn't feel anything. It was especially hard to pretend when Nazir was so damn honest. He allowed me a second to overthink—or try to put the pieces together—because he wanted me to know how he felt. His honesty had always been a turn-on for me. I hated myself for craving his honesty like oxygen.

Shaking off the feelings that kept creeping up my spine like a chill, I picked up my drink again and took a sip.

"You don't get to sit here and say that."

He leaned forward, his forearm muscles flexing against the edge of the table. "Why not?"

"It's been years, Nazir. We're not those people anymore or in that place. We've both moved on."

As much as I was turned on by his honesty, it had me taken aback. Although what I had said was true, I didn't expect him to agree.

"You're right. We're not. But everything I have felt for you, Tata…that shit didn't just die because my stupid ass decided to leave."

I slowly looked up into his eyes, too nervous to use my drink as a distraction. It was like I was seeing him for the first time—really looking into his eyes and seeing past my own hurt that I felt every time he stared at me.

The same man who loved me before he knew how to extend that same love to himself. The man who was trying to be everything that *I* needed him to be. A man who couldn't let me down, so he decided it would be better for him to leave than see the pain he would cause.

My fork slipped from my hands, making a loud clattering sound through the quiet restaurant. The low music did little to hide the sound of my plate and fork clashing against each other.

He leaned back into the booth, eyeing me down with that same gaze that always made me feel like I was standing in front of him naked.

"Finish your food," he finally said. "I'll walk you back to the room."

The waitress came over to check on us, and I ordered another drink. She was quick and had that drink back to me in less than five minutes. I kept requesting drinks while eating my food. Nazir continued to watch me, like only he could, while slowly eating his. The first drink was strong, and I felt a little tipsy. The second and third drinks sealed the deal. They told me I was going past my limit, but I ignored it.

I needed several drinks to sit across from this man.

When the check came, she placed it toward the center of the table and started using that infamous little scraper to clean every last crumb from the surface. Stupidly, I reached for it, and the daggers he sent were enough to make me put my hand back under the table.

"Tata, don't ruin dinner. Alright?"

"How would I ruin dinner?"

Hearing the slight slur of my words, I thought it would be a good idea for me to shut the fuck up.

He put his credit card into the black leather folio and handed it back to her.

"Why the fuck would I make reservations here for you and expect you to pay? I know you got it, and that shit is sexy to me... always been sexy. You've always been kept a certain way, and with me, it's no different. I know that wasn't the case in the past."

Just then, someone came from the back. He must have been very important because other diners were discreetly pointing as he made his way toward our table. He smiled, introduced himself to me, then held his hand out, and he and Nazir embraced.

"Give me a few minutes, Tata."

I took a long sip of my drink. "Take your time. I know how to get back to my room."

He looked at me, giving me those eyes that told me to stop playing with him. I watched as he swaggered away, leaving his phone and wallet on the table.

I couldn't understand why my heart and mind were at war. My heart kept reminding me that this man couldn't be trusted with my heart again. He had shattered us, and although we were able to pick up the pieces, some were still missing.

The pieces that were missing, I believed he held them.

My mind was telling me that this was Nazir. The man I could trust with anything and who had never let me down. If he disappointed me, there was a reason. He wouldn't have intentionally hurt me. The part that scared me more than my heart and mind at war was the fact that I wanted to trust him again.

After he finished his conversation, he helped me up, and just like when we first arrived, he placed his hand on the small of my back as we made our way out of the restaurant. We didn't even make it to the restaurant's lobby before the liquor started telling me to get slick out the mouth.

Maybe it wasn't the liquor, but years of pent-up anger. So much had gone unsaid for so damn long. With drinks involved, it was inevitable that something was going to slip. The calm exterior I had perfected over the years would slip, and I would come undone right before his eyes.

"How was dinner, Tata? You want something else?" he asked, his hand still on the small of my back, his cologne lingering.

"Yeah, I would have wanted you not to leave, but you did that already," I mumbled as I picked up my pace.

Despite increasing my pace, my four steps were one step for Nazir.

"Never said that."

His calm, nonchalant attitude infuriated me. I don't know why, because that had always been him. In a room full of men puffing out their chests and acting arrogant, there was Nazir—in the corner with a drink, quietly observing his surroundings. Even though he wasn't the loudest in the room, his presence was commanding.

Sexy.

Kept you drawn to him.

Like now, I was furious with him. Yet, I wanted to tear his clothes off and have him right here. I craved his touch, his lips on every part of my body.

"You never have to say anything, Nazir. Calm Naz...always breaking hearts but keeping it cool, right?" I flapped my arms, forgetting I was holding my clutch.

It flew across the small courtyard that separated the restaurant from our hotel. He went over to where my bag had landed and picked it up, holding it for me.

"You had too much to drink, baby."

"*Baby*?" I said in disbelief. "You look at me like that, take me out to dinner like I'm supposed to forget everything. How you left me and didn't care. How am I supposed to act like everything is normal when you ripped my whole world apart, Nazir?"

A couple walked by giggling in the distance. The woman looked at her man in a way that I once looked at Nazir–so in love and sure of who I was giving my heart to.

"Girl, if you know like I know...run from that nigga!" I hollered, and Nazir came over and pulled me toward the hotel.

"Yo, you need to chill," he said, with a hint of amusement in his tone.

His body was pressed against mine as he guided me through the revolving doors, making sure we remained close as it turned to bring us inside the hotel.

"What are you doing? Why are you stopping me? I need to warn her of the mistakes that will haunt her years later when she's staring into her little girl's eyes, knowing she lied to her."

"You think it was easy for me?" He spun me around when we stepped out of the revolving doors. "Tatiana, you are crazy if you don't think I didn't die every fucking day after I left you—that I didn't spend every waking moment thinking about you."

The laugh that escaped me was unrecognizable. It was laced with bitterness and came out quicker than I intended.

"Nazir, I think you moved on just fine. I think you slept well at night, while I was stuck trying to put together the pieces of my heart you shattered. It's funny how you're in my face, but you have a girlfriend and a daughter. Worry about them."

He looked past me.

The accusation that he slept well and went on with life perfectly had hit him. Not because it was true, but because I had no idea how much he struggled. His body tensed, and his eyes shifted further away from mine.

His voice lowered as he finally looked down at me. "You don't know shit about what I've been through. You have no idea how many times I wanted to come back and fix things. How many nights I couldn't sleep because I was worried about you."

He swiped his hands over his face, as if trying to wipe away everything we had just said.

"Well, you stayed away, so you weren't that worried," I shot back.

"Staying away was what was best for you. It was the least I could give you when I had nothing to give."

"Fuck that and fuck you! You left because of your fragile ego. You left because you couldn't handle a woman having more money than you. You never let me help you, always would have rather strugg—"

"A real nigga ain't gonna pull his woman down with him. Why the fuck would I take you from a life where I knew you would be taken care of and safe to make you struggle? Staying would have meant introducing you to struggle—a life that was beneath you. I wouldn't have been a real man if I willingly led you into that life."

"So, now because you have money, you think you can come get me back? Bullshit. I am not even that kind of woman."

"I don't expect you to fall into my arms and everything will be fine. Tata, I know I fucked up, and I own that shit. You have every right to hold that pain and hate for me. I fucked this up… fucked you up."

"I'm not that same girl you left in that bed, Nazir. I will never be that girl again." My voice cracked as I stared into his eyes.

Ugh. I was so damn angry with him. We were both strangers, not really knowing each other. Why did he have to leave me? I didn't want him to be a stranger. I wanted him to be who I had always known him to be.

Nazir.

His hands found mine and held them. My heart did somersaults in my chest as I looked up at him. Tears threatened to spill down my cheeks, ready to ruin my makeup.

"I don't want her," he said, his voice rugged and rough. "I want you. Exactly as you are— however broken you believe yourself to be. But I'm not leaving again. I'm going to fix you. I broke it, so it's up to me to make it right by loving it back together."

He rubbed my chest, and my heart melted.

My body grew warmer as I kept staring up at him, speechless. In that moment, I could feel the earth slowly spinning on its axis. Why did he have to say the right things? I hated how I wanted to believe every word he said to me.

Without saying another word, I spun around and headed deeper into the hotel toward the elevators. I didn't need to look back to know that he was right behind me. The touch of our hands and the intense stare told me that he felt the same way.

We both felt everything.

CHAPTER FIFTEEN

Nazir

WHEN WE FINALLY made it upstairs, her stubborn ass fumbled with the keycard, hands shaking, instead of letting me help. Standing behind her, watching her fight with the door and keycard was triggering for me. It was triggering because, in a sense, I had left her alone to fight. All those years, she had to push her feelings aside and fight without me there. She had to become a new mother while mourning a love she never thought she would have to mourn.

After she cursed under her breath the second time, I gently moved her out of the way and used mine. I stepped back, and she staggered toward the door. I gently grabbed her wrist to steady her. It was gentle enough that she could have slipped her wrist out of my hold if she wanted to.

She turned to face me, her eyes misty from wanting to cry. I hated to see her cry, and I wanted to hurt anyone who made her cry. What did you do when you were the person who caused those tears?

I didn't give either of us a minute to think or plan what to say next. When she didn't fight to get out of my grasp, I pushed her against the door and kissed her. Our bodies collided; the kid was hard and almost desperate.

As if I had spent every waking moment planning how this kiss would go, I slowed down, and she melted into me like I knew she had wanted to do from the first moment she saw me. Her hands bunched up my shirt, wrinkling it in the process—but fuck that shit. I didn't care.

She pulled me closer, as if she didn't want me to slip away again. I held her waist, pulling her closer to me as I prepared to slam the door. Her body pressed again mine felt like everything I had dreamed of since she had been missing from my side. Every curve, every soft whimper she allowed to escape from her lips filled me with enough energy to take on the world.

"Sweet Love" by 112

After closing the door, everything became a blur until her back hit the wall next to the door. My mouth stayed locked on hers, as if I was sending apologies through every kiss. Telling how sorry I was, and that I would never hurt her again. Promising her forever, because this time, I wanted to give her forever and every day after that.

Her hands found their way around my neck as I remained bent down, our kiss still locked in, as if neither of us wanted to detach from the other. Finally, I broke our kiss and pressed my forehead against hers, both of us panting and wanting the same thing.

"I should have stayed. Should have fought for you…us," I breathed out.

I could feel her hands trembling at the back of my neck. She was nervous. I softly pecked her lips before resting my head back on her forehead.

"You didn't," she whispered back, her voice cracking in the process.

"I know," I rasped. "But I'm here now, Tata. Put that on my life and our kids. I'm not going anywhere."

It would have to take the entire Lower East Side to get me to leave her. I wasn't going anywhere, even if she hated me for it. She stared at me, eyes searching for the truth. She wanted to believe me, but was hesitant because she knew what believing in me had gotten her the last time.

Instead of words, she used both her hands and pulled my face toward hers. Our lips crashed into each other's, like she was giving me a physical forgiveness. Letting me know what she needed, and to let the other shit go—at least for tonight.

I knew that no matter what happened tonight or the day after—Tatiana was mine again.

Her kisses become hungrier and reckless, knocking the air out of my lungs. I didn't need to think or hesitate; I knew what she wanted. I grabbed her thigh, lifting her up as if she weighed nothing, while she wrapped her thick thighs around me like she had been waiting for this moment all night.

Her nails clawed at my back, scraping the back of my neck and sending a shiver down my spine. I sucked on her lips as I maneuvered through the suite to her room. Our lips stayed locked together as I kicked the door open. I didn't give a damn that my shoe might have damaged the door. I also didn't give a damn about my phone ringing in my pocket. All I gave a fuck about was *her*.

She released a soft whimper against my mouth as I hiked her up, holding two hands full of ass. Her ass was soft like putty. Smacking it, I sucked on her lips while still holding her up. I never wanted to put her down. A nigga wanted to keep her right there—rested slightly above my dick that was fighting to be released from my pants. It knew who was near and how much we craved the feeling of her sliding down onto us.

Her soft whimpers did something to me. Made me feel like she needed this just as much as I did. I grabbed at her dress, pulling it up so I could slap her ass without the silk in the way. I yearned to hear her say that I was hers—that this dick belonged to her.

"Fuck, Tata," I breathed against her lips, pressing her against the wall in the room.

The bed was only a few feet away, but I didn't want to let her go yet.

She ran her fingers through my beard, her eyes glassy, panting with anticipation. Her eyes roamed my face as if she was trying to memorize every feature, like she wasn't going to see me again.

The tear dared to be defiant and slipped down her cheek. I caught it with my thumb and held it there while gazing into her eyes.

"I'm sorry," I said, my voice breaking. "I'm so fuckin sorry, baby."

Neither of us moved to say anything. We were both caught up in a silent conversation, never breaking eye contact. I kissed her again, slower, deeper, like I wanted her to feel how sorry I was.

Taste the sorrow I had felt through the years from walking away.

Her tongue slipped into my mouth as she continued to run her fingers through my beard, holding my face with her small hands. I groaned when her tongue went deeper into my mouth. As our tongues danced, I sucked on hers slowly while she moaned into my mouth, unable to take what she was dishing out.

Moving us from the wall, I went over toward the bed and gently placed her onto the bed, my body reluctant to let her go.

She held onto me, staring up into my eyes, wanting to know what would come next.

I could tell that she desperately wanted me to lead her. Tell her where I wanted her. How much I needed and craved her. How I dreamed of the way her pussy felt on my dick. The gushing sound it always made. Tatiana never got wet for me; she flooded for me. Opened the dams and moisturized my dick with her juices.

Removing my shirt, I tossed it to the side of the room. She remained on the bed; lust filled her eyes as she took every part of me. Her hands reached up and slid down my bare chest, tracing the ink that now covered the old tattoos she used to kiss slowly. The heat of her skin caused my body to tremble, making me look like I couldn't handle her.

I couldn't.

This wasn't a regular fuck. It wasn't one of those times when I drop dick into a shorty and send her on the way. This was my future—the one who I let get away. So, this was different for me.

I pulled up her dress, which was bunched at her waist, and slid it over her head. Stretch marks covered her stomach and sides from carrying life. Her breasts sat perfectly on her chest. They weren't as full as I remembered.

They had nursed a child.

My child.

While other women were out there displaying their "Build-A-Body" physiques, her body remained as natural as I remembered. My lip trembled as I took in her body and quietly moaned. Tatiana did something to me, and she didn't have to do anything or say a word.

I was in awe.

She stood there naked, not cowering or giving off any signs of self-consciousness. She owned her new body. The body that had birthed life, gone through life, and powered through. My baby was proud of her body.

"I told you I'm not that same girl anymore," she whispered.

I bit my damn lip while staring at her. "You're all woman, Tata...fuck."

My eyes refused to move from the art that was in front of me.

My breathing increased.

My heart pumped.

She was breathtaking.

Years had passed, women had come and gone, and she was still the most beautiful thing I had ever seen.

"Say something, Nazir," she whispered.

"You killing me, Tata," I said, my voice coming out so rough that I didn't recognize it my damn self.

"Tell me," she pleaded.

She wanted me to lead her, tell her what I wanted her to do. Her eyes told me that she needed me to dominate and give her direction.

"Play with that pussy for me, Tata."

I stood over her, my legs shoulder-length apart, and watched as she fell back onto the bed. Her legs opened, and I internally screamed while watching as her fingers found their way inside her and swirled around in the wetness. Then she removed them and stuck them inside her mouth, sucking them clean while staring right at me.

"Like this, Naz?"

I bit my lip and nodded. "Stop playing and show me how you play with that pussy."

I backed up until I was leaning on the dresser and watched as her fingers went to work. How she turned herself on and moaned while she continued to tease herself—one hand in her pussy and the other rubbing her nipples.

"Add another finger. I know you remember," I demanded, and she squealed, doing exactly what I ordered.

"Hmmm," she moaned as she played with herself like a DJ spinning a record.

It was taking everything in me not to run from the dresser and get in the bed with her. There was something about watching her please herself, with her eye contact directly on me. I imagined that she had done this many times before while thinking of me, but now I was here in the flesh.

I quickly removed my sneakers and slowly approached the bed. Every step I took, I lost a piece of clothing until I was back standing directly in front of the bed. I lowered myself until my nose was between her legs. Taking the longest whiff, I moved her hands and kissed her pussy lips.

"I missed you, Tata."

She remained quiet.

"Dreamed of the day when I could feel you and taste you again."

Flicking my tongue, I got a reaction out of her. The soft moan let me know she heard me, that she was listening because I meant every single word. My mouth slowly sucked and pulled at her lips as her body squirmed around on the high thread count sheets provided by The Valora.

When her legs started to shake, I sealed it with a kiss and slid myself up until our bodies connected, becoming one. As I slowly entered her, she held my shoulders and eye contact. I kneeled down to kiss her lips. She buried her face in my neck, whispering my name and begging for what was to come next. It wasn't about sex tonight; it was about marking my territory. Reclaiming what had always been mine.

I wasn't that boy from our past. I was a man, and I wasn't running.

The second I felt her on my dick, I lost the small amount of self-control I had been preserving. She was lying underneath me—her hair wild, lips swollen from kissing, and skin flushed. Her eyes followed mine, telling me that she had only ever needed me.

Wanted me.

My forearms found comfort on either side of her head, trying to breathe through what I was feeling. My body wanted to jerk and send her to the moon, but I needed to savor this moment.

Her soft hands slid up my arms as she kissed my shoulder. I pulled back to stare down into her eyes. Her perfectly manicured hand traced an old tattoo she used to tease me about back when shit was simple for us. I watched as her finger lingered over one of the new ones she hadn't noticed—the one inked after I thought I had lost for her. She stared at the tattoo, like she could feel all the hurt I carried when I got it.

"Tata..." I whispered, my voice filled with emotion.

She blinked back tears, some clinging to her lashes but not falling yet.

"Nazir...I don't want to think about any of that. Make me forget tonight."

"I want this more than I wanna fucking breathe, but I need to know...are you sure?"

Even with me already inside her, even though every part of me wanted to put her through this mattress, if she told me she didn't want this, I would've pulled out of her, and the feelings would have remained.

She nodded, her hands messing in my beard. That was all the confirmation I needed. I kissed her like I wanted to pull her lips from her face—slow, deep, and with the right amount of roughness. Each peck of the lips was me pouring into her—telling her how much I had missed her, how sorry I was, and how I loved and never stopped loving her. With her legs wrapped around me and her hips arched up, she invited me further inside of her. I couldn't rush this and nut. I needed to feel her, make this moment last longer.

Preferably forever.

I pulled out of her and replaced my dick with my hand, palming her pussy and feeling Niagara Falls. She was so fucking wet that I needed a caution sign.

"Baby, you so fucking wet. I missed how wet you get for me. Fuck, baby," I growled and shoved all of me back inside of her.

Her body jerked, she gasped, and I watched as her mouth fell opened while I pulled out and thrust back in. I felt her nails dig into me, her soft whimpers turning into loud moans. Her hair stuck to her forehead as I held onto the headboard with one hand and her hip with the other, delivering thrusts that made the expensive bed slam against the expensive wallpaper.

"You trying to kill me, baby."

She let out a soft moan, adding a chuckle. "Then die slow."

Fuck.

Her wit and comebacks had always been my favorite thing about her. A prissy private school girl from Greenwich, who had a mouth like a sailor and could suck dick like a porn star. I was willing to die slow if that meant I could hold onto this nut that I knew both of us were snowballing. It was moving slowly, accumulating more power from both of us, and the urge was becoming stronger. Sliding the head of my dick through her pussy slowly, I teased us both until her hips lifted, wanting even more of me.

"Harder, Naz," she panted, scratching my back harder.

I pushed in harder, letting her feel every inch of me stretching her, filling her, and connecting us back together. My dick continued to swell at the pain of her nails in my skin. I softly kissed her lips as she adjusted her body, making our bodies mold together. Because being fucking real, they had always belonged together.

"Shit, baby. You still feel like mine," I gritted, pushing deeper into her, sending her legs up.

Her hands framed my face, pulling me down for a kiss that almost fucking broke me. I moved inside of her slower, dragging out every stroke because I didn't want it to end. Trying to carve every memory I had of her into her vaginal walls. She met every thrust with soft moans, gasping, and whispering my name that made me lose my shit each time she said it.

There was no rushing. We didn't need to because we had waited and prayed for this. Envisioned this moment when it didn't seem possible. This wasn't about me busting a nut; it wasn't about fucking. This was about earning her trust, showing her how much I desired her, and coming together as one again.

This wasn't perfect; it was messy. Our mouths had missed each other's mouths a few times, and her pussy juice was on my knees. Both of us trembled because this didn't feel real. Pulling out of her, I stared down at her juices on me, reminding me that I was *inside* of her. This shit wasn't another wet dream.

I kissed Tatiana from her forehead to her neck. Any place I felt deserved a kiss, I kissed her there. Sucking on her neck, I continued to deliver slow strokes that had her tossing it back at me, letting me know it felt just how she wanted it to feel.

"You feel so fuckin' good, baby," I spoke into her shoulder, as her arms held me around the neck tighter. "Missed this...missed us, Tata," I admitted to her.

She clung to me tighter, her tears falling freely. "Me, too."

"Say what you mean, and mean what you...say, beloved," I growled lowly in her ear, watching the hair on the back of her neck stand.

"I...I missed you, too, Nazir," she moaned back.

Hearing her tell me that she felt the same way shattered me. It made my heart hurt because she spent so much time missing me. We had spent so much time missing each other. Missing out on a life together, kids, and a marriage that would have made my parents proud.

"I'm not going nowhere, baby. You believe me?"

Her body tightened, and the pitch of her moans became higher as her nails dug deeper. I felt her coming before she could say anything. Her walls caved in, becoming tighter while pulling me in. Her breaths were labored as she bit down on my shoulder, screaming in the process.

"Zirrrrrrrr!" she screeched as she came down hard.

I felt her body jerking in my arm before she went limp. Her eyes remained closed tightly as her breath calmed down, and her legs around me loosened. My name fell from her lips like she had screamed it into her pillow, wanting me.

Needing me.

I increased my speed. The sight of her reaching her peak had me ready for mine. My lips brushed against her neck while I felt myself about to go over the edge. Holding her in place, I spilled inside of her.

We both laid there sweaty, breathing hard, and fucking pulled apart and undone. Still, I remained inside of her, resting my forehead against hers. She couldn't move, and I damn sure couldn't move. Fuck, I didn't want to move. This wasn't just sex for us. It was tension that had been building during our time away from one another.

Anger.

Love.

And regret.

This shit felt like redemption to me—like she was welcoming me back and letting me know I couldn't leave her again.

On my seeds and even the unborn ones, I wasn't going to let her go again. Leaving wasn't an option, and I needed her to know that.

I was home.

CHAPTER SIXTEEN

Yaya

THE CITY'S LIGHTS *lit up the dark room. Even though I had closed the balcony door, I left the curtains open. The light illuminated Jonah's face as he continued to stare at me. All emotions were out in the open, so the room was quiet. Everything felt calm right now, and I embraced that.*

I needed calm.

Jonah remained on the edge of the bed, one hand resting low on my back like he wasn't ready to let me out of his arms. He wanted me to stay right here because the second I moved, all of this would be a thing of the past. As if he knew it would never happen again if he let me go.

Neither of us said a word. We didn't need to. Our breaths were enough as we listened to the faint hum of the central air in the room. I slowly removed myself from his lap and crawled over toward the place I had been sitting before he pulled me over toward him. I pulled my legs up to my chest, hugging them tightly. My oversized shirt slipped off one shoulder, and before I could fix it, his hand reached out and gently pulled the fabric back into place.

His fingers brushed against my bare skin, sending shivers down my spine. It was how gentle he was that caused that pesky-ass lump to appear in my throat. I tried to swallow it back down, but staring into this man's eyes was emotional for me.

Allowing anyone to see me like this felt raw. Like I had opened my front door and allowed anyone to come in. I've been someone who went through things alone, and when I needed someone, it was always Tatiana.

I felt exposed, transparent, as if he could see right through me. I wasn't the Yaya who he flirted with and shared playful banter. He saw me as a mess, a wreck that needed to be fixed. I wasn't as controlled as I appeared.

"You good?" he asked, his voice rough like he hadn't used it in a while.

He cleared his throat and looked over for my answer.

Wiping my face, embarrassed to even be in this situation, I nodded my head. "Yeah."

He removed himself from my side of the bed and walked toward the other side. The bed dipped when he sat down. Putting his back against the headboard, he spread his long legs out.

"You don't gotta be good for me, Yummy."

I smiled. "You are sticking with that nickname, huh?"

He ignored my question. "You don't always have to hold it together all the time. With me, you can break, fall apart, and I promise I'm gonna hold you together so the pieces don't fall."

It pained me how much those words broke me all over again. Hearing him tell me that he would be strong for me. Hold me together if I needed him to, and he didn't want anything in return. He didn't want me to hurt and continue to be the strong person. Jonah wanted to be strong for me. He wanted to show me that it was okay to feel shit and allow those emotions out.

I remained quiet for a while, picking at my shirt, pretending like the thread unraveling was more important than this conversation. Without thinking, before I could get inside of my head and talk myself out of it, I shifted closer to him. My breath was barely coming out, as I listened to my heartbeat through my ears. I had gotten so close that our arms were touching.

I rested my head against his chest and listened to the steadiness of his heart. He didn't move; he allowed me to become comfortable on him. He let out a breath and wrapped one arm around me, tugging me closer into him.

My eyes became heavy, and all I wanted to do was rest. Quiet my mind so I could sleep peacefully. I felt him kiss my head, so soft and gentle that had I been asleep, I would have missed it.

"You don't have to say anything, Yummy. Just let me hold you tonight."

We didn't need to dissect what was happening, and I was grateful for that. He wanted to hold me, and I was going to let him do that. I curled into him, his skin soft against my cheek. His scent drove me wild.

His hands found their way to my ass, and he gently rubbed my ass in slow circular motions, forcing my eyes to close and sleep to find me. The sound of his calm heart and the motion of his rubs had me snoring seconds later.

I had zoned out behind my desk, a stack of papers scattered around. As if I didn't have a ton of work, I had been daydreaming about Vegas and that moment between me and Jonah. That night kept replaying in my mind on a loop. It was all I thought about, and if I could, I would go right back to that exact moment.

"Glad that you have joined us again."

Tatiana's voice forced me to look at the doorway, where she was leaning, watching me.

I started messing with the papers on my desk. "How long have you been there?"

"Long enough to be concerned."

She took my question as her invitation to enter my office and make herself comfortable on the chair in front of my desk.

"There's no reason to be concerned. I am, however, concerned about you rushing us to leave and not telling Nazir that you were leaving."

The morning after the meeting, Tatiana came to my suite with security and told me that she was going to leave. Made some excuse about wanting to get back home because she had a lot of work to do. It was less about the work and more about something else, but she refused to talk about it. All I knew was that I found myself rushing around my suite to pack my clothes so we could catch a commercial flight back to New York. Jonah came out his side of the suite when I was almost done.

Tatiana refused to tell either of us what was going on, and since he still had meetings in Vegas, he couldn't leave to come with us. As long as we had security, he was cool with us leaving. Emilio was going to be at the airport to pick us up the moment we landed.

"Why would you be concerned with me? I'm doing amazing," she said, crossing her legs and trying to act nonchalant.

I stared at her for a second longer, making her uncomfortable. "You fucked him."

"What?"

I pointed my finger at her while squinting my eyes. "You had sex with Nazir, and now you are avoiding him."

From the way her ass was over there fidgeting, I could tell there was truth to what I had accused. Tatiana had been keeping herself busy since we had been back from Las Vegas—spending as much time as she could with Zira while also working a lot.

Nazir hadn't been to the house, and when he did pop over, Tatiana was never there. She was either at the spa or somewhere in the house, avoiding him.

"You sound crazy. I should be concerned about you and Jonah."

"He comforted me after our conversation we had. Allowed me to lay on him, and it felt good. I don't know how I feel, or if it even means anything. Now you go."

"We had sex, Yaya. Sex that had me feeling like I could forget what the hell happened. It was so deep and raw that I had tears. He had me crying while he was making love to me...'cause that's what he was doing. Showing me that he never stopped loving me."

I was less interested in the incoming call from Sav that I quickly silenced and was more concerned with my friend. "And then you left him the next morning. Pretty petty if you ask me."

"I found myself sleep, Yaya. Actually sleep in his arms, and I couldn't do it. I couldn't allow myself to fall back into it with him. I can't trust that he won't leave again...leave me high and dry."

"You don't even believe those words yourself."

She crossed her arms. "How do you figure?"

"You wouldn't have allowed him in. He wouldn't have been able to make love to you if you didn't trust him. I think the problem is that you trust him, and that scares you. How could you trust a man who abandoned you... That's the thought that scares you."

"It's not crazy of me to have those thoughts, Yaya."

I sighed and leaned on the desk. "You're not crazy to have those thoughts, but you are crazy to jump in bed with him knowing the history you two have together. That wasn't two people hooking up after a few drinks. It was two people's souls connecting again."

"I made sure to take a Plan B soon as I got back," she added.

"And raw? Gurl."

"He has a girlfriend and a daughter," Tatiana blurted.

I paused. "Seriously?"

"Yes, and he never confirmed or denied it. I'm so dumb at times. Why would I give myself to him knowing these things? He moved on and had a life without me."

"You did, too...even if it was an arranged marriage. You could have divorced Karim, but you fell in love and lived a life with him. I'm not saying that Nazir wasn't a thought, but I can bet he wasn't as important in your life as he used to be. He was allowed to move on and have a life, just like you went on and had one."

"Then why is he telling me how much he missed me and loves me, but has a girlfriend?"

"You just said that he didn't confirm it, so why are you assuming he has one? What if he just has a baby mother?"

"That's even worse," she groaned dramatically.

"How long do you plan on avoiding him?" I wondered.

She shrugged. "Until I can act normal in front of him. The way he sexed me, I don't see me being able to keep my cool around him. Actually, we don't need to see each other ever."

"The drama. Sheesh."

She laughed. "All I know is that I need to focus on other things. Have you reached out to the realtor? It shouldn't take this long. Does the seller even want to make money?"

"I have that on my list of things to do today. While we were in Vegas, I called and left a voicemail with him."

"Cool. Lunch later?"

I looked at the time, and then back at my best friend. "I think I'm going to take a ride to visit Sav. I haven't seen her in a few weeks, and I know today is the day for free visits."

"You pay to visit her?" Tatiana said with pure disgust.

"No. Today is when you can go without having to schedule and get approval. It allows other felons to be able to see their loved ones. It's only an hour drive, and I can see her for a few."

"Well, if that's how you want to spend the rest of your day." She rolled her eyes and pulled herself out the chair.

I snorted. "You choose to fuck and hide...and I'm choosing to see my girlfriend for a few hours."

"Don't even do me."

"Nah, you already let Nazir do that," I teased, and she tossed a balled-up paper at me as she left my office.

I quickly answered a few emails and called the realtor. When I received his voicemail, I left him another message before grabbing my things to make the drive to the prison.

On the drive to the prison, I turned on my favorite Keyshia Cole playlist and sang with my entire heart. I was singing like I had been betrayed and cheated on, when I was the one laying on a man's chest in Las Vegas. It was the guilt eating me up because I wasn't that kind of person. I didn't do shit like that.

I was a faithful partner and Sav never had to question if I was out here doing her wrong. I mean, she never had to question, but that never stopped her ass from doing it. She always accused me of doing some shit, which is why I was out here feeling guilty.

She was out her accusing me of doing her wrong and look what she caused. My ass went ahead and did her wrong. Laying on a man's chest wasn't that wrong. Except we both knew that it was wrong. Receiving booty rubs from a person who wasn't my girlfriend was wrong on so many levels.

Jonah was only comforting me and trying to make me feel better. It was innocent, and I needed him to hold me because I was overwhelmed after the conversation with Tatiana. Actually, this was all Tati's fault. Had she not gone all deep with our conversation, I wouldn't have been emotional and needed to be comforted. Then again, the kiss that I placed on his chest as he slept peacefully the next morning wasn't right either. I watched as he slept, his eyelashes sweeping his face, as beautiful as ever. God handcrafted this man with his bare hands.

I pulled into the visitors parking lot and killed my engine. Sav drained my energy so bad, and I knew this visit would do the same. By the time I left, I knew I would need to drink at least three bottles of wine to have a decent sleep.

It had been a while since I had come to visit Sav, so I knew she was going to bring it up. I would have to sit there and listen to how selfish I was, and how if the roles were reversed that she would have come to see me every week. It was bullshit because if the roles were reversed, I would have gotten a decent lawyer and accepted the help that was being given. That was neither here nor there. The fact remained that I had to walk up in here and listen to her bullshit.

After going through security, I finally made it to the visitation room with questions. The guard had marked it down as a family visit instead of a single visit like it usually was. Whenever they marked it as a family visit, it was more than one person visiting.

Visits were already underway when I finally finished with security. I scanned the room to look for Sav, but I couldn't find her. I heard a laugh, and that's when my head snapped in that direction. I saw her sitting with her locs pulled back with a rubber band; her smile was infectious. I mean, I couldn't deny how beautiful Sav was. Her light skin covered in different shades of tattoos, and her perfect white smile.

Her teeth were always my favorite thing about her, and now she was smiling in some bitch's face. I couldn't see her face because her back. However, Sav looked up briefly, and that's when our eyes locked.

"Oh shit." I read her lips as I casually walked over towards the table. There was no need for me to act an ass. This was a female prison, and I didn't want to end up in there with her ass.

"Hey baby," I greeted and sat beside the woman.

Sav avoided eye contact like a muthafucka. She was trying to look everywhere but into my eyes.

"W…what you doing here, Yaya?"

"I can't visit my girlfriend? You're always on my neck for not making time, and I make time and here you are on another visit. This a cousin or something?"

The woman was stunning, and I couldn't deny that. She had golden brown skin, soft curls framed her face, and her body was curvy. Even with her being curvy, I could tell she wasn't all that tall.

"I'm not a cousin. Who is this, Savannah?"

Oh, she was using her full name. I had been screamed at for calling her by her real name, and this woman just openly said it without it being a problem.

"Come see me tomorrow, Yaya. Not the time for this shit."

"Why would I ever come back tomorrow when we can get everything out on the table now. Hi, I'm Yalina…" I allowed my voice to trail, waiting for her to extend her hand to shake mine.

It took her a minute, but she finally did.

"Hi, I'm Natalie…Savannah's fiancée."

I wanted to scream, punch her in the throat, and then pull the fire alarm. Instead, I remained seated and gave her a tight-lipped smile.

"Oh really?"

"Yaya, come the fuck on."

I took a deep breath. "You know what…I should have fucked Jonah in Vegas. Should have allowed him to take me to the moon with his big dick. Instead, I settled for a hug and comfort when we both know I wanted to ride his dick."

Her jaw flexed because she was bothered. As much as this woman was seated beside me, claiming to be engaged to her, the thought of me with another person was too much for Sav.

"Why the fuck you choosing to cut up right now?" she replied through gritted teeth.

Sav was so mad that I could see steam coming out of her ears.

I laughed. "I wasted so many years on you and held you down when everyone told me to leave you. Literally every person in my life has said that I needed to cut you loose, but I didn't. Too loyal to leave you because yo' funky-ass mama didn't love yo' gay ass. Sav, go to the deepest pit of hell, and forget that you ever knew me. I'll make sure your shit is sent to your cousin's house, and my number will be changed by the time I get back on the turnpike."

I didn't need to stay to hear her excuse or to hear what Natalie had to say.

For all I cared, Natalie and Savannah could be together. I would probably send a wedding gift. That was how fed up I was. My heart raced as I left the visitation room as quickly as I came. The tears didn't start until I reached the parking lot.

Fuck Sav. I never needed her, and it was time for me to realize it and actually believe the shit.

CHAPTER SEVENTEEN

Tatiana

"Been That Way" by Bryson Tiller

I SAT IN bed with a glass of wine on the side table working through the night. It was a little after ten when I finally washed the day off my body and climbed into bed. My fingers glided across my keyboard like butter on toast as I confirmed a few meetings like it wasn't the early hours of the morning.

My digital clock slowly waited its moment to turn four o'clock. I continued to work as I listened to my favorite Pandora channel lowly, careful not to disturb Nazira while she slept next to me. She randomly had those nights when she wanted to be close to me, and I never fought her on it.

There would come a time when all she wanted was time away from me, so I soaked up the moments where she just wanted to be my baby. I smiled at her as she made a little snorting noise. Lightly brushing her hair from her forehead, I placed a few kisses on it before shutting my computer down and climbing out of bed.

My alarm would soon ring, reminding me that I needed to work out before my day started. Routine was what kept me in order, so I tried hard never to stray from the routine that helped with mourning the death of my husband.

Lately, my workouts were less about routine or my late husband and more about Nazir Kane. I was trying to work out to forget about the night we shared a few weeks ago. I wanted to desperately forget that night. Like our last night before he left, that night was now forever etched in my brain.

The way he catered to my body, reminding me how much he loved and missed me. Reminding me that no other man would make me feel this way. Even with Karim being dead, I felt guilty because he had never been able to get that kind of reaction out of me.

Karim and I had a healthy sex life, and it was amazing. However, it wasn't like what I expected with Nazir. Years later, and this man still owned my body, and he knew it. When he pushed inside of me, he knew that he controlled me. I was torn between hating it and loving it all at the same time.

Aside from never being able to sleep much, I was becoming frustrated with my realtor about the second location. After seeing the location before Vegas, I knew I wanted it, but he hadn't moved on giving us any more information on it. He was using the excuse that he was out of the country to hold us off.

Rex thought Yaya was beautiful, so she was always able to get anything out of him with a simple bat of her eyelashes. I knew things were bad when he wasn't answering the call for her. This second location for Hush was so important to me because it would bring new energy. It was something Karim would have wanted for me, and I always wanted to make him proud. Our Greenwich location generated a lot of revenue because so many people traveled to us. With a location right in the city, I knew the buzz would be everywhere.

I quickly did my morning routine and changed into my workout clothes. Instead of going to work out with Yaya this morning, I was going to work out in the home gym. I didn't need her pressuring me to talk about what I had going on. All I needed was to run on the treadmill with my headphones and thoughts.

I grabbed my phone and headed downstairs to the kitchen to grab a smoothie from the fridge. My body froze when I saw Nazir sitting at the kitchen island with a bowl of cereal.

He spotted me and continued to eat his cereal. "Good morning, Mrs. Kane."

I paused, trying to decide if I had heard him correctly. He surely didn't call me Mrs. Kane, and he wasn't eating my expensive protein cereal out of a mixing bowl. I had to be dreaming, because that wasn't what was taking place right in front of my eyes.

"Nazir, what are you doing in my home?"

"Security, Tata. Emilio been working around the clock, and the nigga needed a break." He shrugged like this wasn't crazy.

"I…I don't even know what to say," I stammered, no longer concerned about the smoothie I couldn't wait to have seconds before. "There are other members of security that could have filled in for him."

"Why the fuck would I do that when it's a man's job to protect his wife?"

"What the fuck? Nazir, you sound crazy."

He shrugged, getting up to put his bowl in the sink. "Nah, I sound like a nigga that had some of the best pussy and ain't letting up on it."

I stood by the fridge, and he moved closer to me. My legs wanted to move, but they were stuck like they had been glued down.

"It was just sex, Zir."

Nazir looked down at me, holding my chin between his pointer finger and thumb. "Not even you believe that shit, Tata. All that whimpering you were doing as I fucked you hard enough to let you know I'm back, but gentle enough for you to know I missed you…us."

A small moan escaped my lips. "Zir—"

My phone ringing interrupted the moment, and I wanted to kiss whoever was calling me. I removed myself from him and went to grab my phone from the end of the counter. Rex's name popped up on the screen.

"Hey Rex," I answered with a shaky voice, trying to control myself and slow down my breathing.

"Um, hi, Tatiana. Is it a good time?"

"Yes, the perfect time. What's going on with the location?"

Rex sighed, which was a sure sign that something was wrong. "It was sold, Tatiana. The buyer offered above asking and didn't want to send in an offer. The seller went with it and didn't consider our offer."

Rex didn't sound like someone who just lost a big commission. I've purchased enough property with him to know when he was pissed that something slipped through his hands.

"Who is the realtor?" I asked.

"Huh?"

"The realtor for the buyer… I want to speak to him and the buyer. The Sterling money is long, and you know I can offer more and buy it from them."

"Tatiana, I don't thi—"

"Call them on three-way, Rex," I replied, not wanting to hear any of the excuses I knew he would have.

"I'm the realtor, Tatiana."

I snorted. "Figures why you're on an island enjoying your new commission. Call the buyer, now."

"He wanted to remain priva—"

"Call that nigga now, Rex!" I barked into the phone, coming out of character because I was pissed with him.

Have I not been his best client and always went through him for commercial properties? Had I gotten my inheritance, I would have purchased more property with him. My father made sure that I got married, which voided me receiving it because I married into a wealthy family. It was a bullshit clause that I didn't think existed. A lot of fishy things often happened when it came to money and Malcolm Rich.

Nazir remained behind me, and his phone started to ring. I bet it was his girlfriend calling to check on him. Rex patched the call on three-way, and I paused when I heard the voice over the phone and the one behind me.

"What up, Rex?"

I ended the call and spun around on my heels to face this fucker. He kept the phone to his ear with a smirk on his face.

"She hung up?"

I reached up and snatched his phone from him. "Rex, you can go to hell. How long have I known you?"

"Tatiana, I can find you something better for half the pric—"

"Fuck you, Rex! I hope you accidentally drink something with mango in it!" I ended the call and tossed his phone across the counter.

Rex and I went to college together and lost touch after I dropped out. When the condo that was beside mine in the city went up for sale, he happened to be the realtor. I didn't get an inheritance, but I received my condo.

"Tata, you can't talk to our family's realtor like that."

I stared at him in disbelief. "I take you as security for you to snake me on a property that you weren't even worried about."

"The property is yours. No strings attached. I can transfer everything into your name by noon," he said all nonchalant, like the property wasn't worth millions of dollars.

I stood there and then stormed off downstairs to the gym. I was going to run so hard that I would have to vomit by the time I was done. What the hell was going on in my life, and why was Nazir in it? He was supposed to be a thing in the past, and he was making me see that was no longer the case.

"Tata…"

I turned as I started stretching, and he was standing there watching me. "You should be with your girlfriend and child. It was just sex, and we both know it should have never happened."

"Why the fuck are you trying to hurt my feelings, Tata?"

I scoffed because he was serious. "*Your* feelings? What about my damn feelings? Nazir, this is crazy. Why are we even having this conversation? You fucked me and then had the nerve to have a little family."

He remained quiet. "You right. I do have a little family."

His honesty shattered me. I expected him to deny it or make an excuse, but he did the opposite.

"Get the fuck out of my house."

"You always had a problem with hearing what you want to hear."

I nearly broke my neck with the way I twisted to look at him. "You held an entire conversation in front of me, and never said anything to me. Fucked me knowing you had a family."

"You allowed me to fuck knowing I had a family."

I couldn't turn and look at him because that was the truth. As a woman, I should have stopped whatever was going on, but

I allowed it. Allowed him to have my body in a way that only he could.

"Won't happen again."

I could hear his house slippers shuffle across the floor. *When the fuck did he get house slippers in my house?*

He kneeled down until he was almost eye to eye with me. "Nazani is my daughter. Natalie is my best friend, and we have a child together."

I snorted. "As if that ever works out. She knows that she's your *best friend*?"

He nodded. "Yes. We dated before she realized that she wasn't you, and she would rather have my friendship than try to compare to a woman who she couldn't compete with."

"What? That sounds crazy."

"May sound crazy, but it's the truth. Nobody has compared to you since I left, Tata. I've been in and out of relationships before I decided to just fuck. It was easier to fuck a woman than to give her what was yours."

"Giving them dick is giving them what's mine," I muttered. "And sleeping with your best friend was the best course of action for you?"

Nazir laughed. "I never slept with Natalie. We kissed a few times, but I never had sex with her. She was special to me, and I knew if we crossed those lines that it would ruin things."

"Nazir, please get out of my damn face because clearly you are playing games with me. How do you have a child and never slept with that girl?"

He finally got down on the floor with me, his legs extending on either side of me. "We had our daughter through IVF. Natalie wanted to be a mother, and I wanted to be a father. We decided to go in half on a baby. Nazani is the best thing that has happened for the both of us, and we co-parent. She knows about you…probably too much."

The words wouldn't come to me because I didn't know what to say. What did I say to an explanation like that? Two friends, deciding that their friendship meant more than trying for a relationship, had a baby.

I don't know if I was more shocked at the fact that he had a daughter with his best friend, or the fact that Nazira had a little sister who had a similar name to hers.

"There's so much that I don't know about you. You come back and expect me to give you my all. Nazir, you never even introduced me to your mother or family."

He nodded his head, understanding where I was coming from. "I was protective of you. Shit sounds like a bullshit-ass excuse, but it's the truth. I wanted to keep you away from that side of my life. You saw me as Nazir, and I didn't want you to see where I came from."

"What we had was fake then."

"You introduced me to your family? Did I sit down and shoot the breeze with Malcolm Rich?"

He had me there. Nazir had been a secret like he made me his secret. I was afraid for the same reasons that he was. I feared my father would judge him and force me to end things. My mother would take one look at him and tell me that I could do better.

Nazir didn't come from wealth, and that was what they expected from me. They wanted me to marry a man who could take care of me, and at that time, Malcolm couldn't do that. I never held it against him, though.

"I never cared about the money, Zir."

"That shit is easy to say when you have money. For me, everything was about money because I had a family to take care of, a father who died in prison…a mother who needed help, and a sister who needed to be raised. So, it was always about money for me. I couldn't take you away from what you knew and introduce you to struggle. Nah, I wasn't going to be that nigga."

"We could have made it together. I'm not so far removed that I don't realize that all people don't live like this."

He stroked my cheek. "The only thing I want to introduce you to is more wealth...never seeing you struggle. I don't want that for my daughters."

It was the way he said "daughters" that made me smile.

"I don't know, Nazir. It's so much."

He kissed both of my hands. "Nothing has to be figured out today. I want to know my daughter, and whatever way you think works is the way we'll do it."

I ignored the call from my lawyer and placed my phone on the machine behind us. "Okay."

"Give me a chance to make things right between us in the process. Let me love you and give you dick until tears spill from your eyes again, baby. Tata, give me a chance to break down those walls."

"Nothing has to be figured out today," I said, repeating his words, unsure if I wanted to grant him permission to break down my walls.

It was because I knew that he would. He would break them down and have me back in love with him. I couldn't deal with that right now, and he respected that.

The softness of his lips caressed mine as he went to get up.

"Mommy?"

I heard Nazira's voice at the top of the stairs. "Yes, baby? I'm working out."

"Can I come down?"

"Yes, of course."

Nazir went and sat on one of the sofas off to the side. I heard her feet coming down the steps.

She noticed Nazir first and smiled. “Hey, twin.”

“What’s going on, pretty girl?”

I melted when he called her “pretty girl” and looked at my baby. She came and climbed right into my lap as I kissed her on the head.

“Did you sleep well?”

It didn’t matter how old she got. She would always be my baby girl.

“I have to talk to you about something, Mommy,” she whispered.

“Okay, is it a secret? Why are we whispering?”

She had a serious expression on her face, and I became serious, too.

“What’s wrong, Zira? You’re worrying me.”

“Mommy, I saw Bloom kissing Pop-Pop,” she replied.

I looked over at Nazir, and we shared the same expression.

CHAPTER EIGHTEEN

Jonah

CARLOTTA CALLED ME hysterical because someone had sold the jet. She was confused because she would never sell the family's jet. Raphael had purchased that jet for their anniversary a few years ago. He knew how much she loved flying down to Boca Raton with her friends, and he figured the jet would make her life more convenient.

That shit showed me that was the exact way I wanted to treat my woman. It was exactly how I wanted to treat Yalina. I wanted to make her life easier, make her softer, and get her to see that her man would handle shit for her.

She knew I was a nigga that took care of business, and she witnessed it with her best friend. I had been here since Karim passed, and I wasn't going anywhere. I was going to handle any problem Tatiana had because I hated seeing her stressed.

That was what I wanted to do for Yalina, while giving her dick in the process. I wanted her to look into my eyes and know that the promises I made to her would never be broken. All she would have to do is make a call, and I would make sure it was handled.

Feeling her body on me while she slept felt like I had hit the lottery. My baby was able to rest without worrying about shit. As pissed as I was that my room had been overbooked, it was meant for me to be in her room that night.

I was supposed to witness her unravel, because she was a woman who didn't come undone. She couldn't become undone because she had too many people depending on her. Aside from her role as Tatiana's assistant, she took on many responsibilities, making sure to provide for her family. Although she was only a few months older than Bloom, she took on the role of the older sister— always trying to direct her to the correct path.

Bloom was free-spirited and did whatever she wanted, while her sister was the opposite. Not to mention the fact that she was holding Sav's ass down while she was locked up. There wasn't anyone to see her unravel at the seams when she was alone. She did that shit on her own, and I was meant to see that. It told me that I needed to apply pressure and show her that I wanted to love her. Shit, I wanted to let my own walls down and be real and open with her, too.

"Jonah, the man I have needed to see. You and Tatiana are hard to get in contact with. Shit."

Joseph Cozzy was the Sterling family's lawyer, and we had become close since I handled most of the things. Usually, we would shoot the breeze and make small talk before handling business. This time, I couldn't sit and have those conversations because I was confused.

"I would normally ask about the kids and shit, but right now, I don't care. Why the fuck was the jet sold?"

Joseph stared at me like I was the one tripping. "Carlotta wanted to sell it. She said the memories made her feel sad, and she just wanted to get rid of it." He pushed his chair out from the desk and then went over to a file cabinet, licking his finger as he flicked through files.

"Why in the fuck would she do some shit like that? Raphael got that for her. She cherishes that jet."

He continued to look until he pulled a paper and then rolled back behind his desk. "Right there…she signed the paper to transfer the sale into Malcolm's name."

I snatched the paper so fast that Joseph jumped back.

"What the fuck do you mean, transferred the sale into that bitch's name?"

"Her signature is right there…even got it notarized. Jonah..." His voice was low as he looked at me.

"Why the fuck are we whispering when I'm ready to set this bitch on fire?"

He looked out the glass, where the other associates and paralegals were staring at us. Joseph quickly hit the button to frost the glass windows.

"Sit down. I have been trying to call Tatiana for weeks now, and she won't return my calls."

"That's because every time you call, she gotta sign some shit that reminds her that both her husband and father-in-law are dead."

He leaned forward, his voice still low. "Malcolm Rich invested all of his money into some Ponzi scheme and lost it all. He's broke and has been for a while. He managed to keep up appearances by slowly selling off his belongings. Before Raphael died, I went to visit him. He told me about all the large amounts of money he found out that Karim was giving Malcolm behind his back."

"Why the fuck would he do that?"

This shit had me about to pull my damn beard out and scream because I was so confused.

"Raphael told Karim to cut him off, because whatever deal they had had been fulfilled, and that was when Karim died a few weeks later. He suspected Malcolm of his death."

My heart slammed against my chest listening to what he was saying to me. "No."

He returned to the filing cabinet and pulled out a folder. "I have been moving some assets into Tatiana's name, because I hate what I'm about to tell you."

"The fuck you talking about?"

"Raphael had a son before Karim was born. He's older than Karim. Raph had him when he was younger. Karim was born before Carlotta and Raphael got married. When you have enough money like Raph did, you can hide and cover things up. His older son is older than him. In Raphael's will, the Sterling fortune goes to his next heir or if his heir has children, which would have been Nazira."

I jumped to my feet and paced his office, unsure if I wanted to hear what would come out his mouth next. Everything he had said had blown my mind. The fact that Malcolm had tricked Carlotta into selling her jet.

"How the fuck was Malcolm able to do some shit like that without Tatiana? Her signature is needed on any sale."

"Raph bought that jet and put it in Carlotta's name. Carlotta has always been the sole owner of that jet," he explained, making me want to lose my shit even more than before.

She trusted his slime ball ass, and he betrayed her for greed. He fucked over his money, so he felt like he was entitled to the Sterling money because his daughter was married into the family.

Carlotta looked at Malcolm like family, and he betrayed her like that. That was the shit that was so fucked up about the entire situation.

I sat back down in the chair, holding the arms while looking at Joseph.

"What the fuck are you trying to tell me? Stop feeding me bits and pieces. Tell me what the fuck is up?"

He hung his head like he didn't want to be the one to break the news, but he had to because he was legally obligated. Raphael treated every person he came in contact with like family. You were family until you proved him wrong. Loyalty was important to him, and even the staff he surrounded himself with knew it. This was breaking Joseph more than I knew, because he was about to say some shit that would change our lives.

Messing with his hands, he looked up at me. "Carlotta and Tatiana have to vacate their homes. I've been holding him off, but I cannot hold him off any longer. He wants everything. All of the Sterling fortune goes to Raphael's older son…Malcolm Aman Sterling–Rich."

TO BE CONTINUED . . .

WWW.BLACKODYSSEY.NET

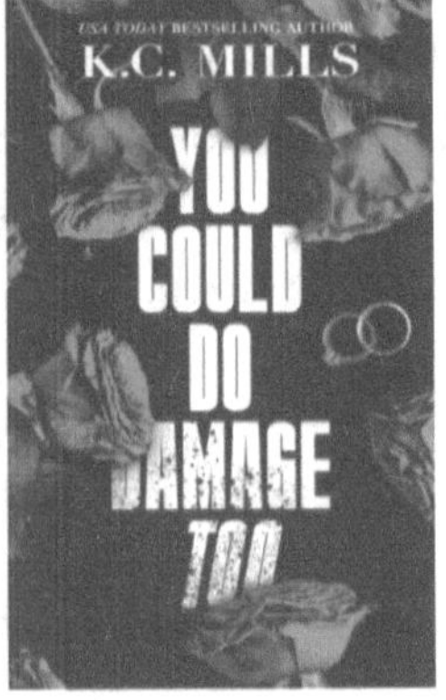

www.ingramcontent.com/pod-product-compliance
Lightning Source LLC
LaVergne TN
LVHW030911080826
845145LV00010B/2849

* 9 7 8 1 9 5 7 9 5 0 8 9 1 *